Figgy & Boone

READY-TO-READ GRAPHICS

LEVEL 1

Best Brother EVER!

Janee Trasler

Dear parents, caregivers, and educators:

If you want to get your child excited about reading, you've come to the right place! Ready-to-Read *GRAPHICS* is the perfect launchpad for emerging graphic novel readers.

All Ready-to-Read *GRAPHICS* books include the following:

★ **A how-to guide to reading graphic novels for first-time readers**

★ **Easy-to-follow panels to support reading comprehension**

★ **Accessible vocabulary to build your child's reading confidence**

★ **Compelling stories that star your child's favorite characters**

★ **Fresh, engaging illustrations that provide context and promote visual literacy**

Wherever your child may be on their reading journey, Ready-to-Read *GRAPHICS* will make them giggle, gasp, and want to keep reading more.

Blast off on this starry adventure . . . a universe of graphic novel reading awaits!

Figgy & Boone

Best Brother EVER!

written and illustrated by
Janee Trasler

Ready-to-Read *GRAPHICS*

SIMON SPOTLIGHT

An imprint of Simon & Schuster Children's Publishing Division • New York London Toronto Sydney New Delhi
1230 Avenue of the Americas, New York, New York 10020
This Simon Spotlight edition September 2022 • Copyright © 2022 by Janee Trasler • All rights reserved, including the right of reproduction in whole or in part in any form.
SIMON SPOTLIGHT, READY-TO-READ, and colophon are registered trademarks of Simon & Schuster, Inc. • For information about special discounts for bulk purchases,
please contact Simon & Schuster Special Sales at 1-866-506-1949 or business@simonandschuster.com. • Manufactured in China 0522 SCP
1 3 5 7 9 10 8 6 4 2
This book has been cataloged with the Library of Congress.
ISBN 978-1-6659-1449-9 (hc)
ISBN 978-1-6659-1448-2 (pbk)
ISBN 978-1-6659-1450-5 (ebook)

How to Read This Book

This is Figgy. He's here to give you some tips on reading this book.

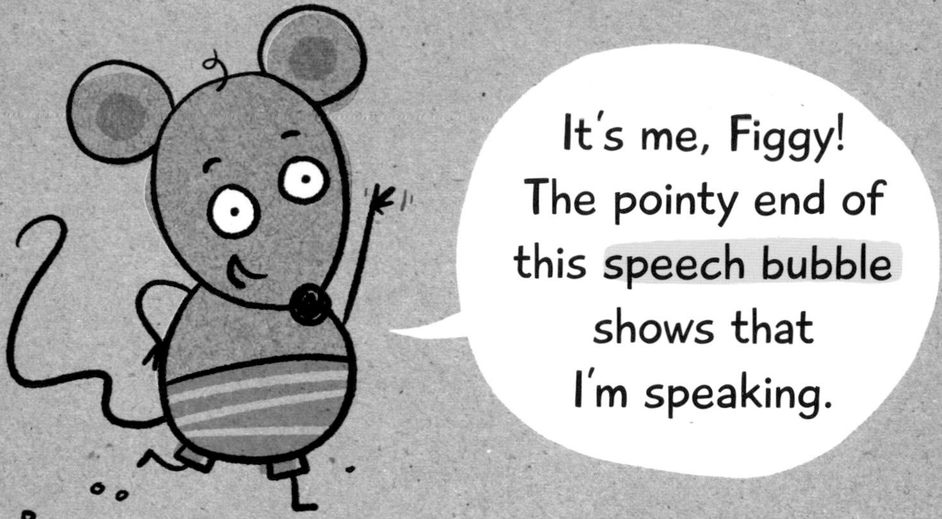
It's me, Figgy!
The pointy end of this speech bubble shows that I'm speaking.

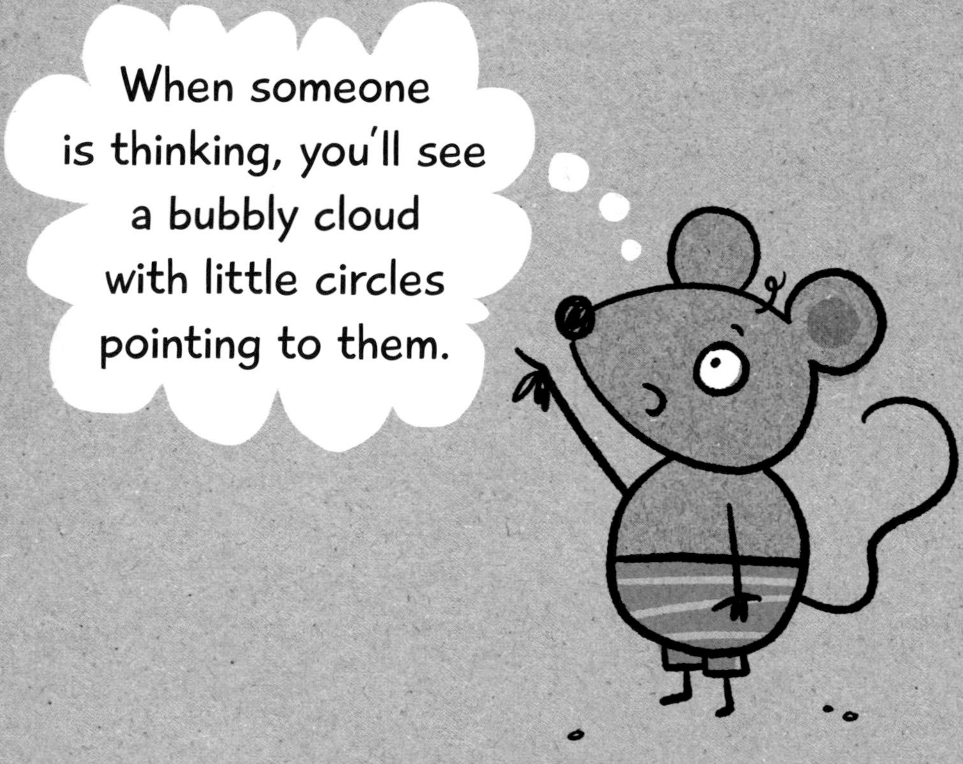
When someone is thinking, you'll see a bubbly cloud with little circles pointing to them.

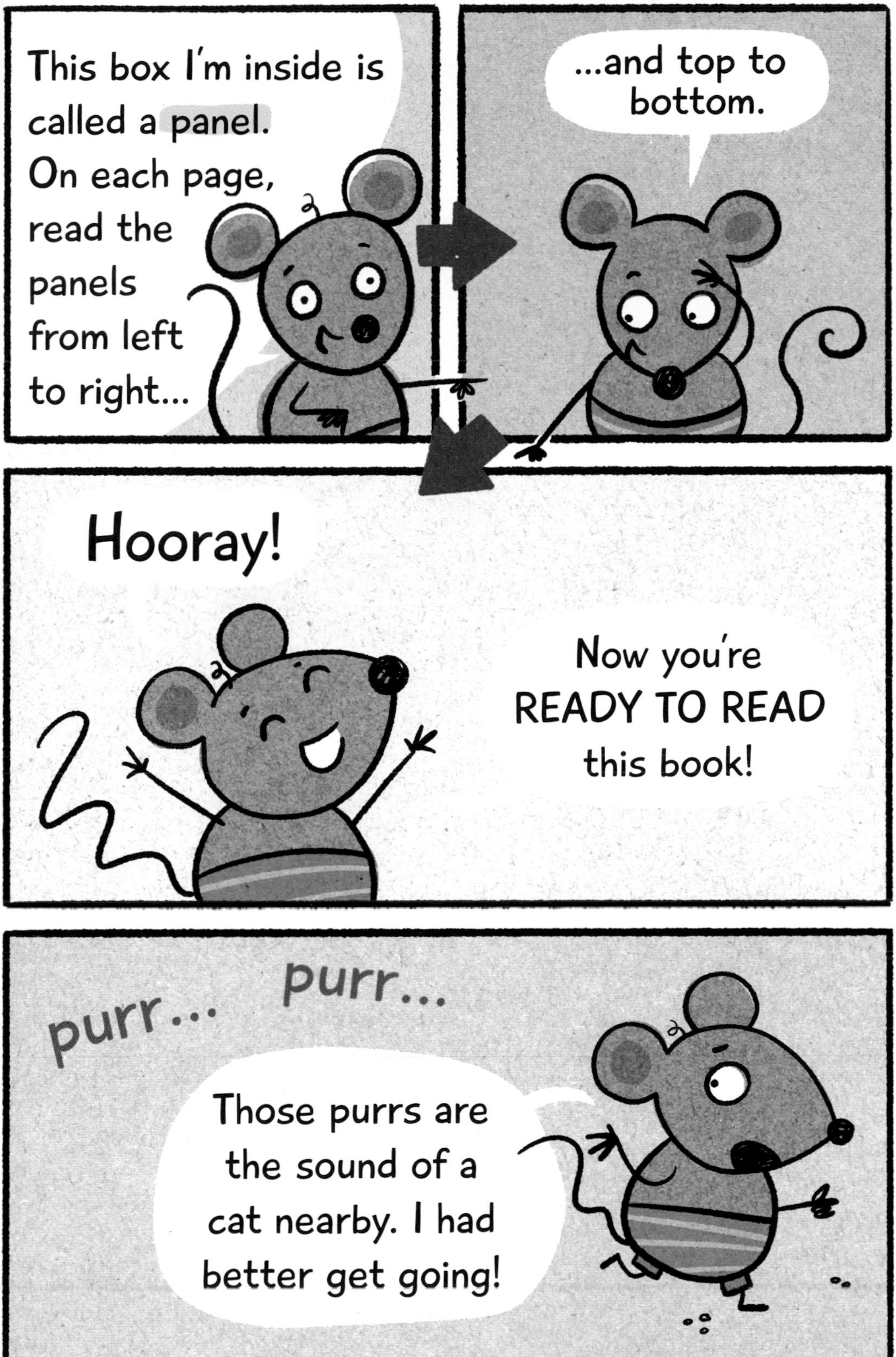
This box I'm inside is called a panel. On each page, read the panels from left to right...
...and top to bottom.
Hooray!
Now you're READY TO READ this book!
purr... purr...
Those purrs are the sound of a cat nearby. I had better get going!

CONTENTS

How to Read This Book   2

Chapter One: **Best Brother**   5

Chapter Two: **Next Brother**   19

Chapter Three: **Oh Brother**   43

Chapter 1
Best Brother

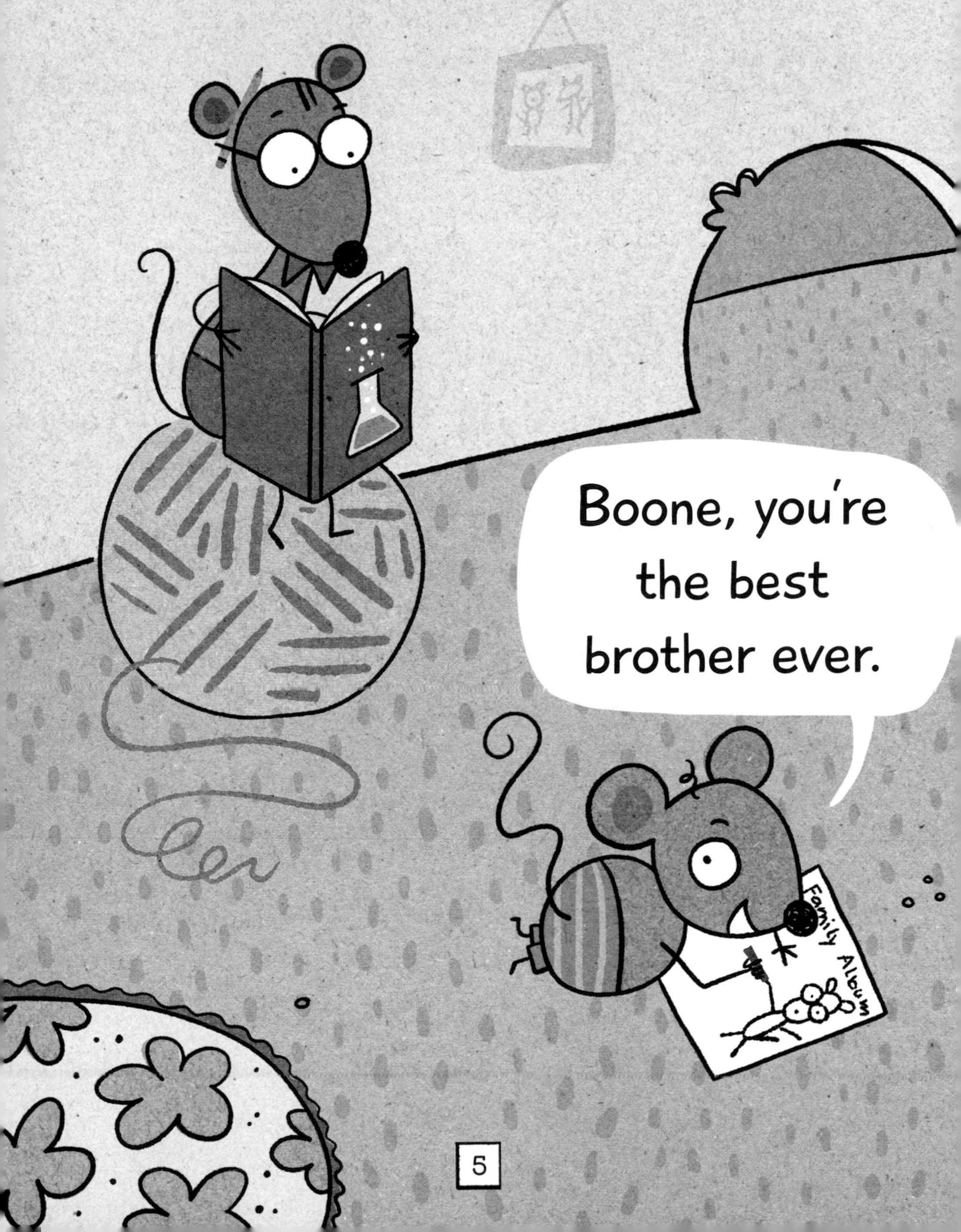
Boone, you're the best brother ever.
Family Album

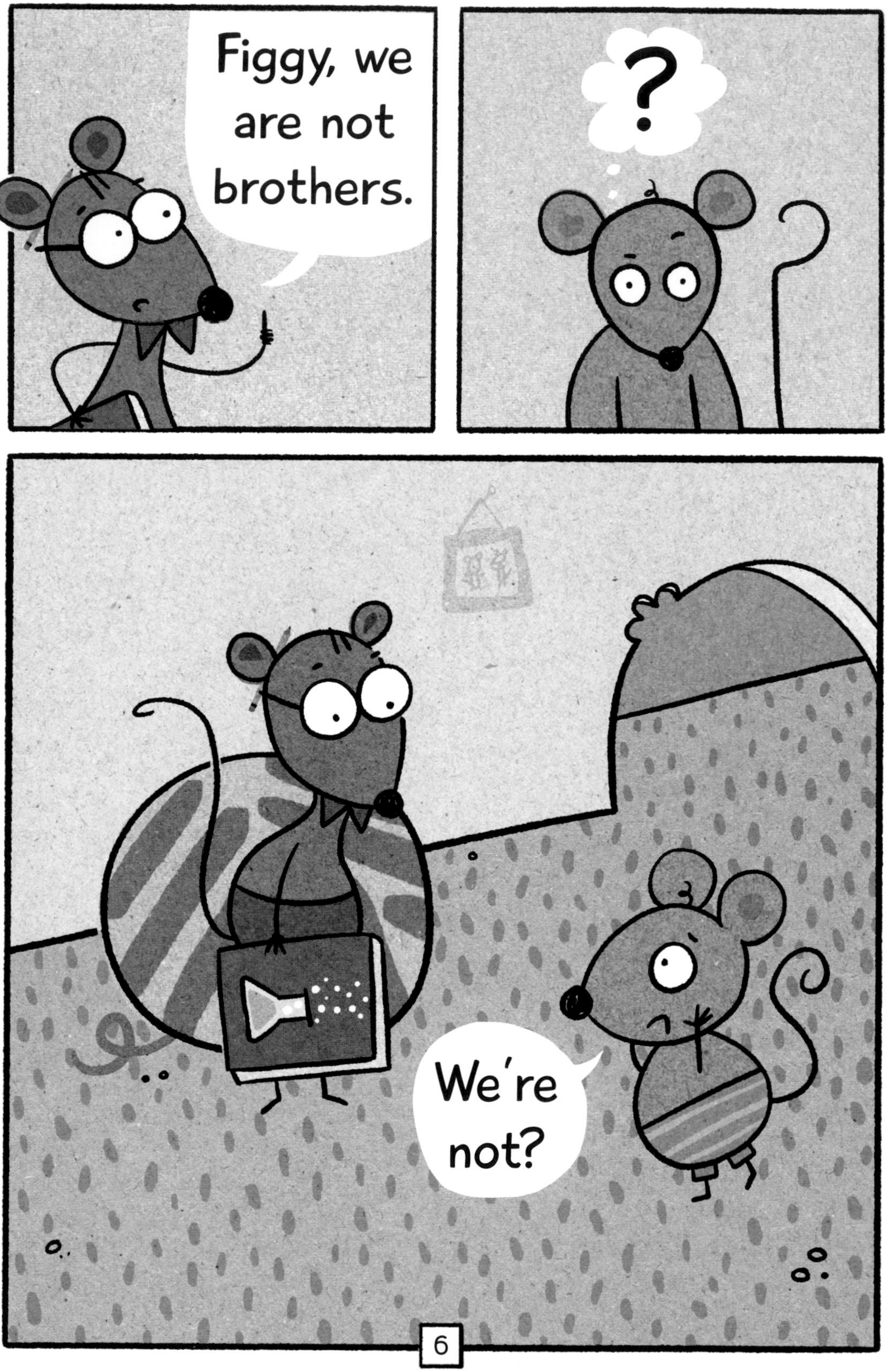
Figgy, we are not brothers.
?
We're not?

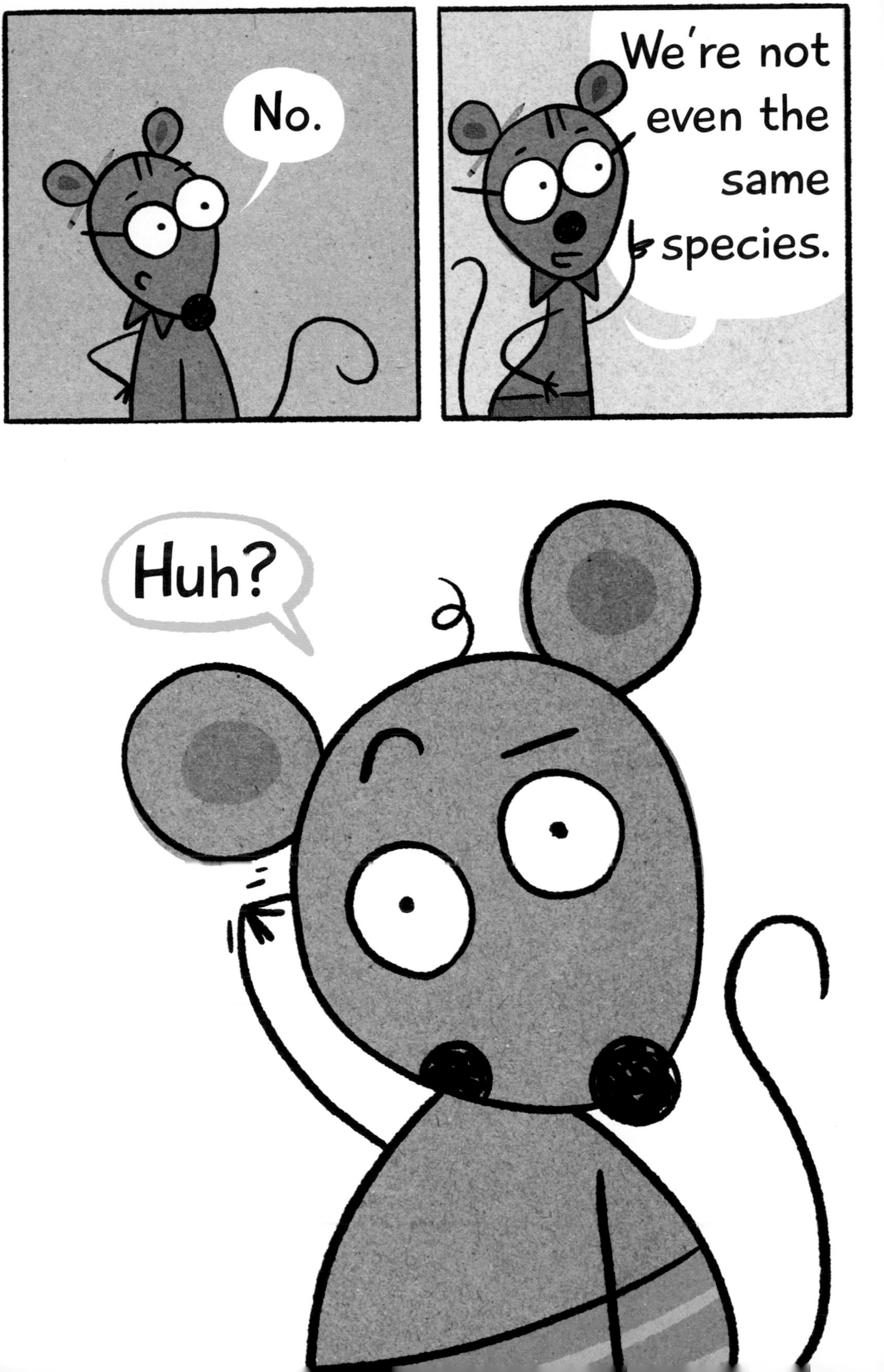
No.
We're not even the same species.
Huh?

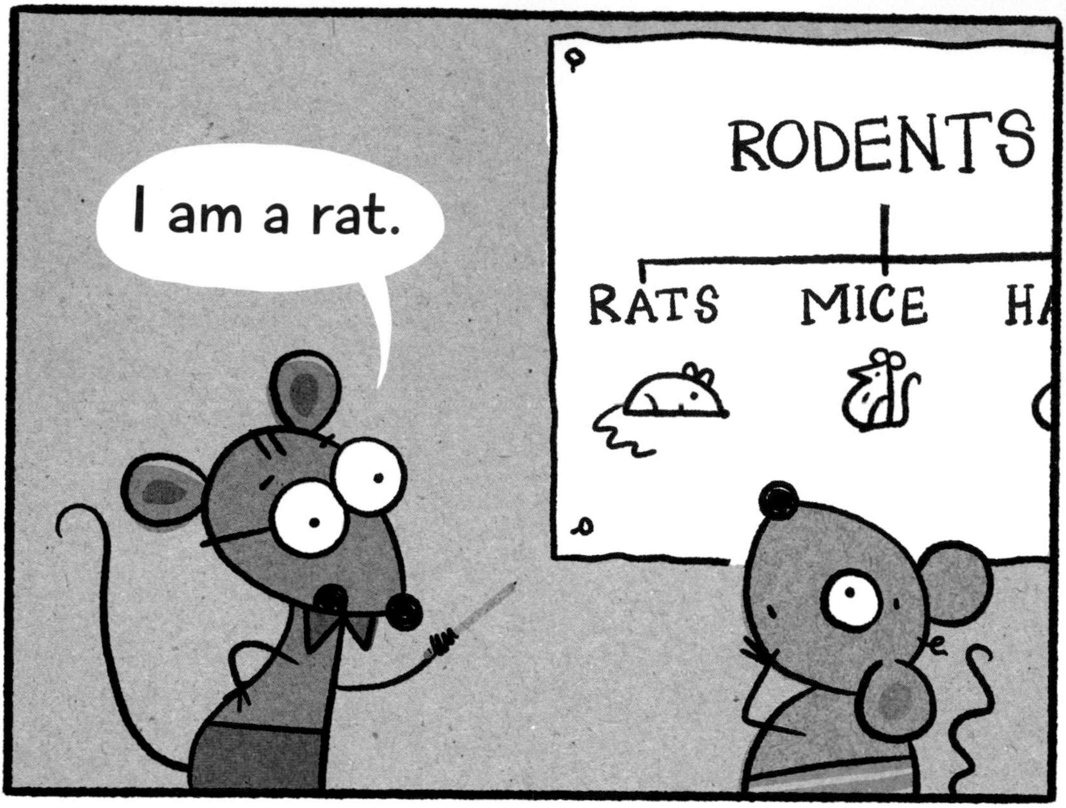
I am a rat.
RODENTS
RATS
MICE

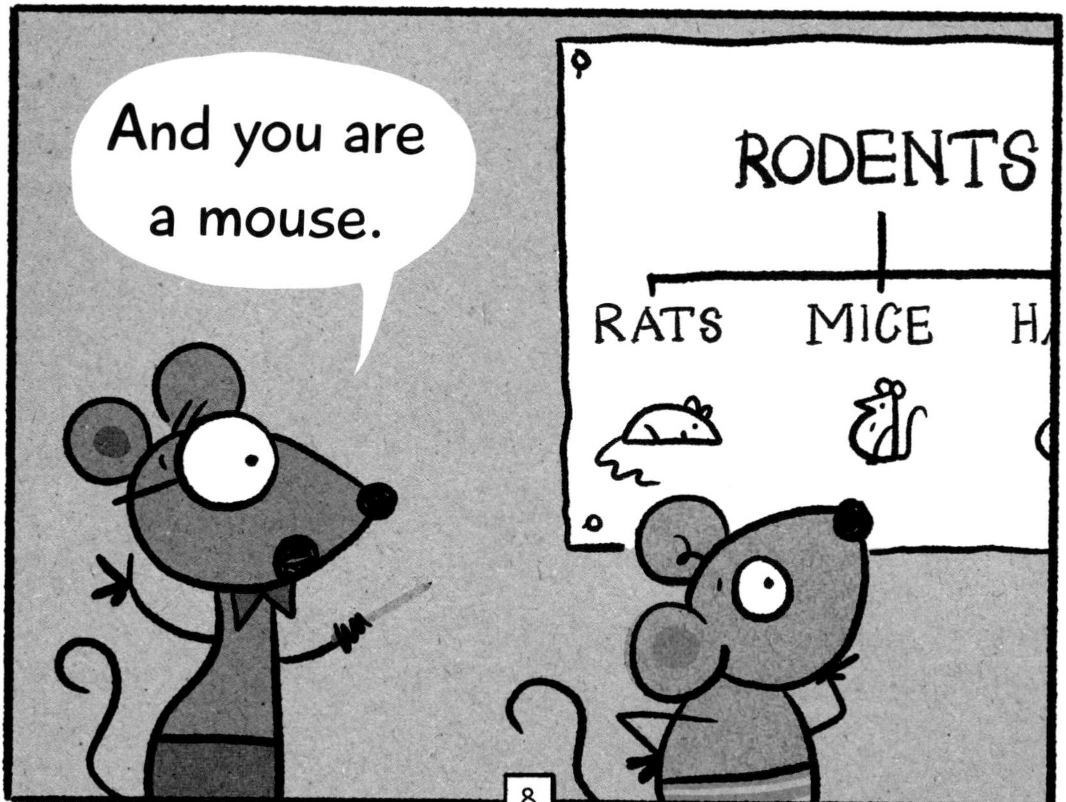
And you are a mouse.
RODENTS
RATS
MICE

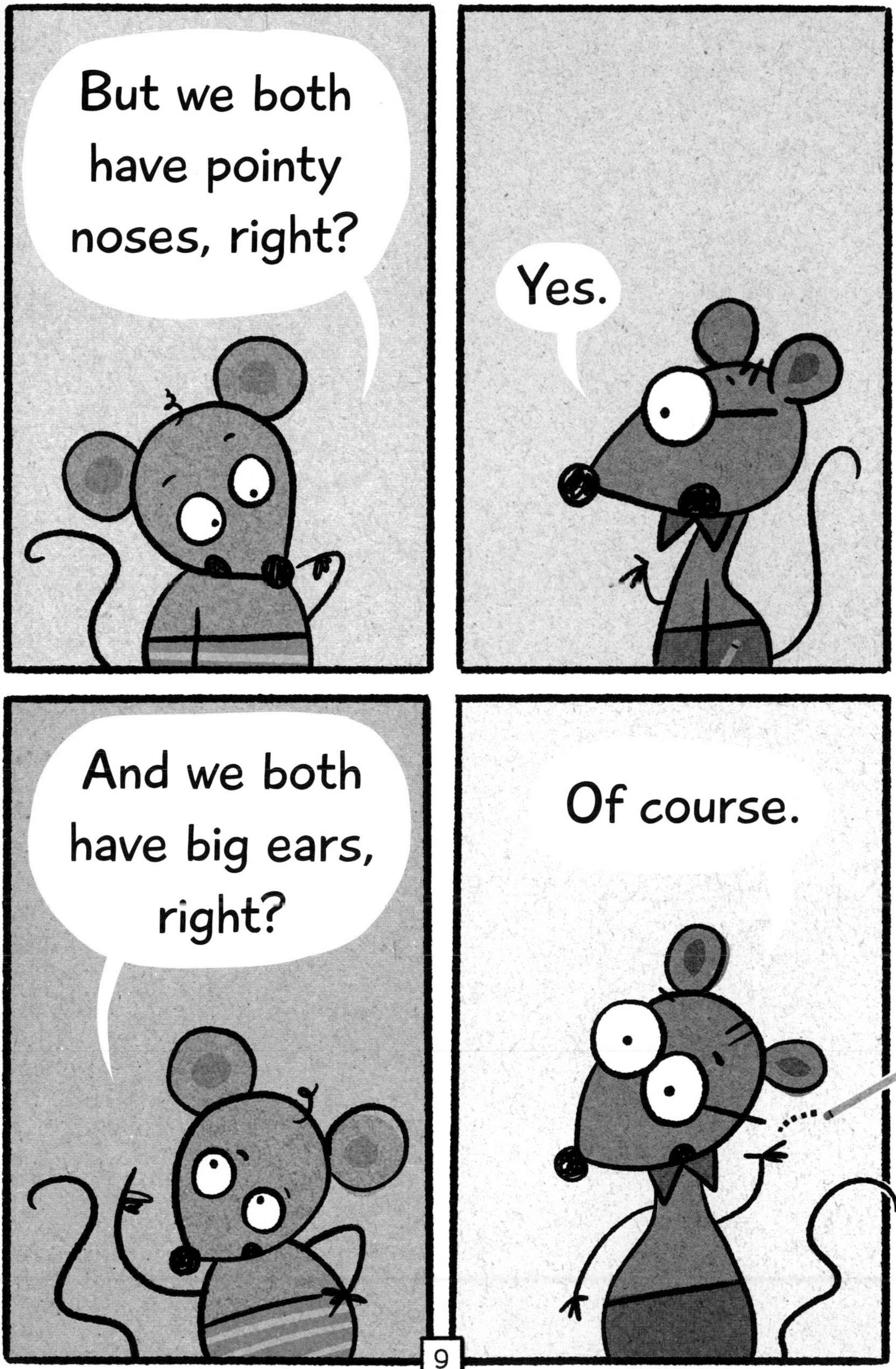
But we both have pointy noses, right?
Yes.
And we both have big ears, right?
Of course.

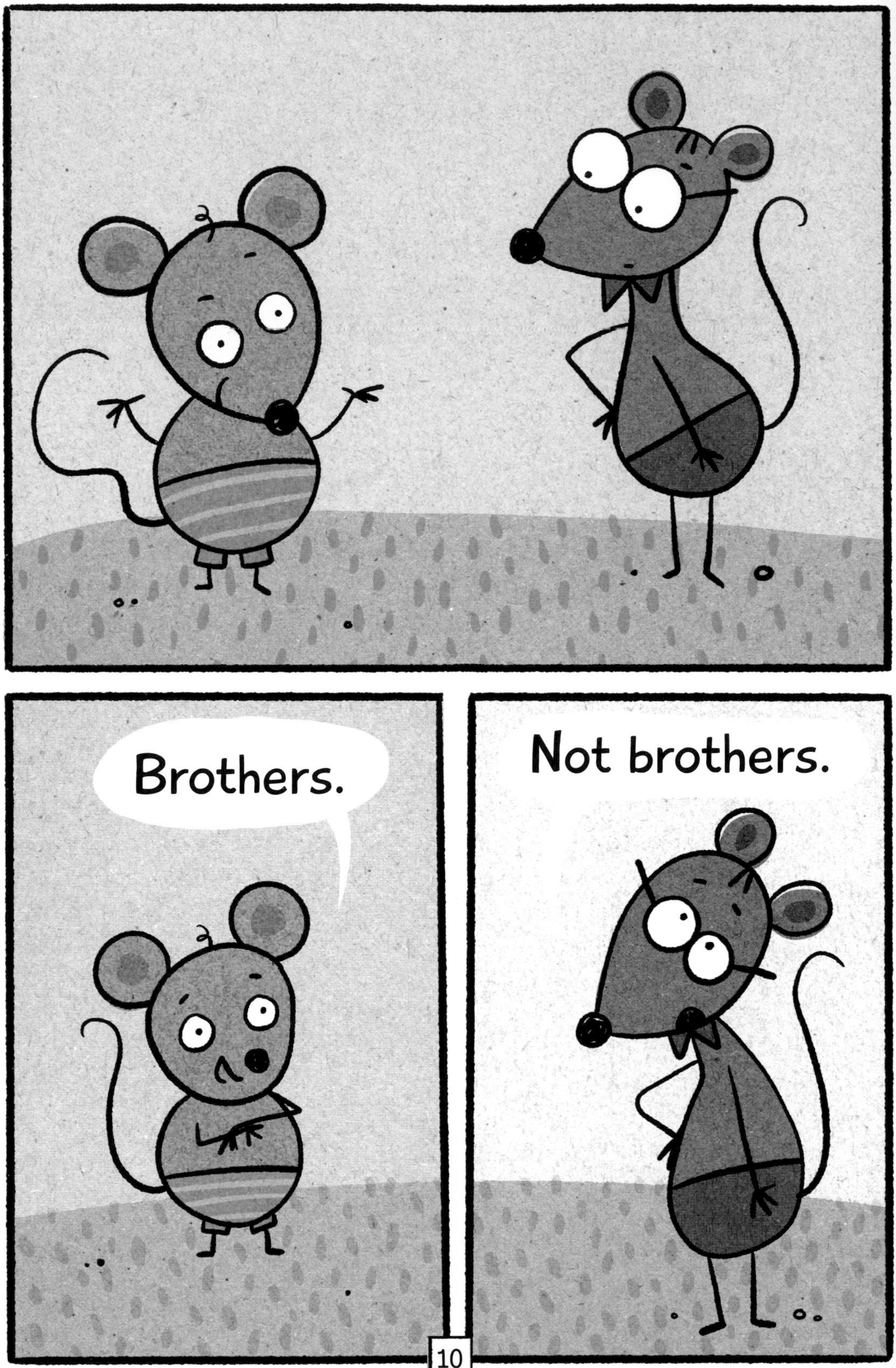
Brothers.
Not brothers.

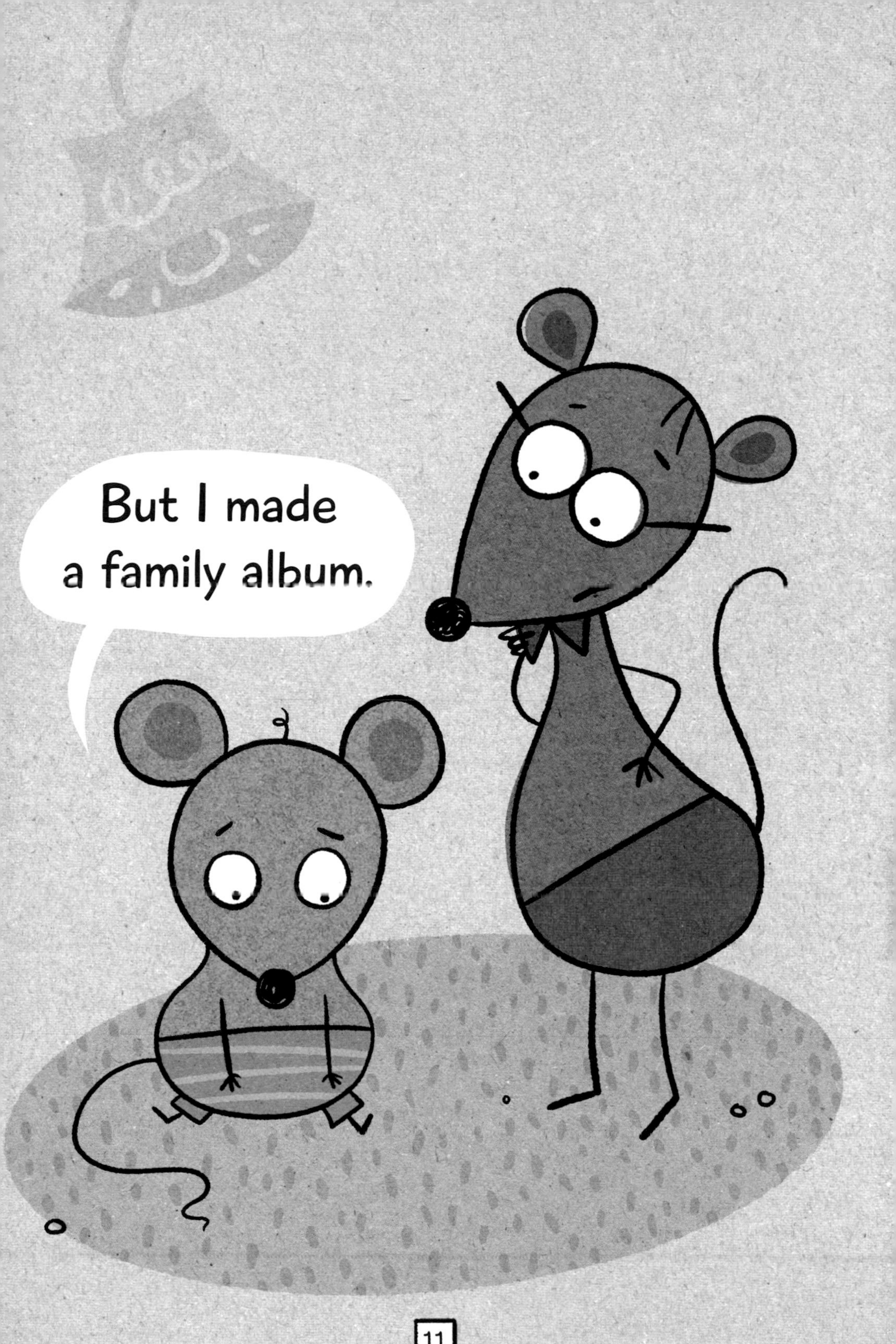
But I made a family album.

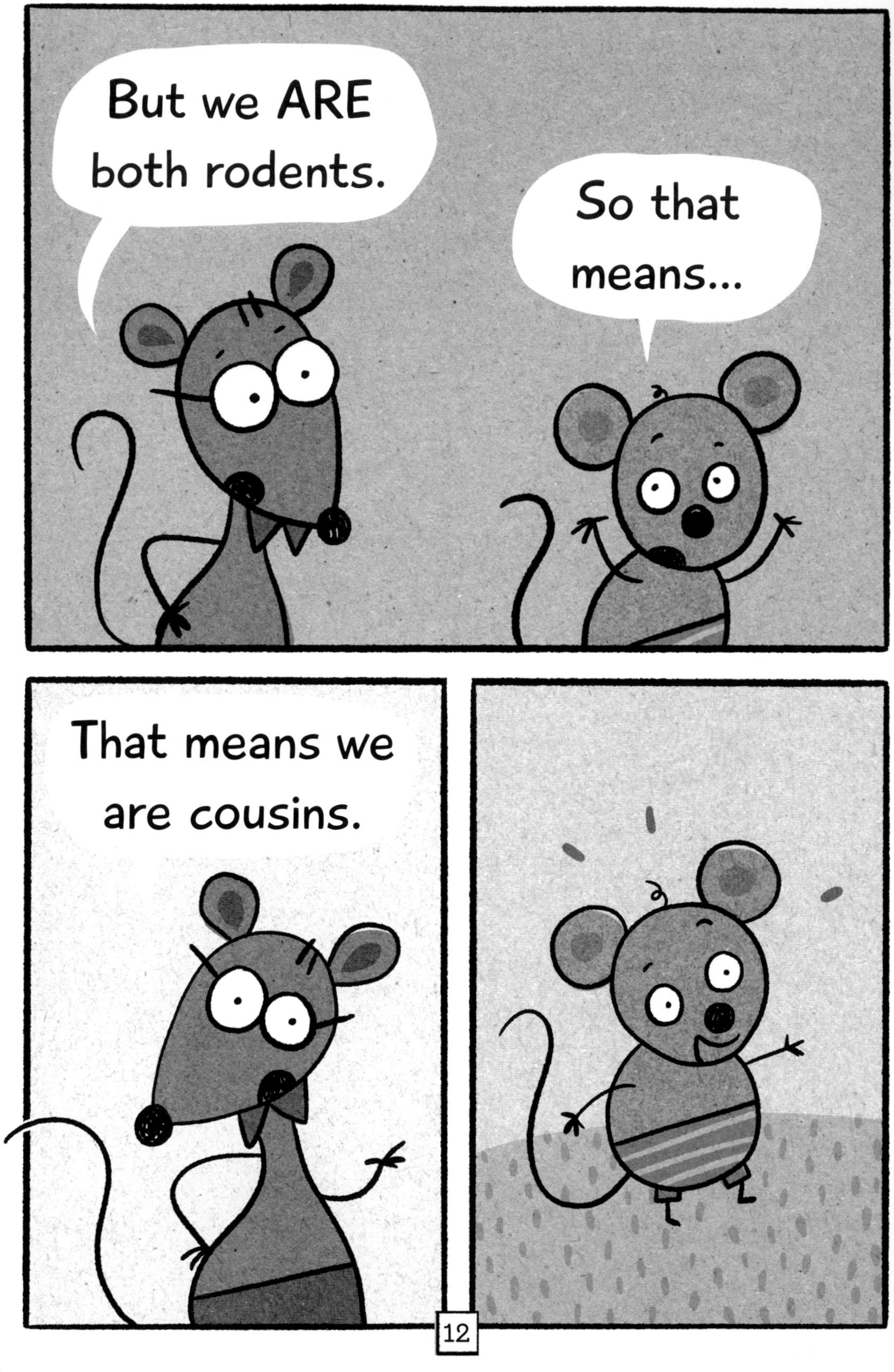
But we ARE both rodents.
So that means...
That means we are cousins.

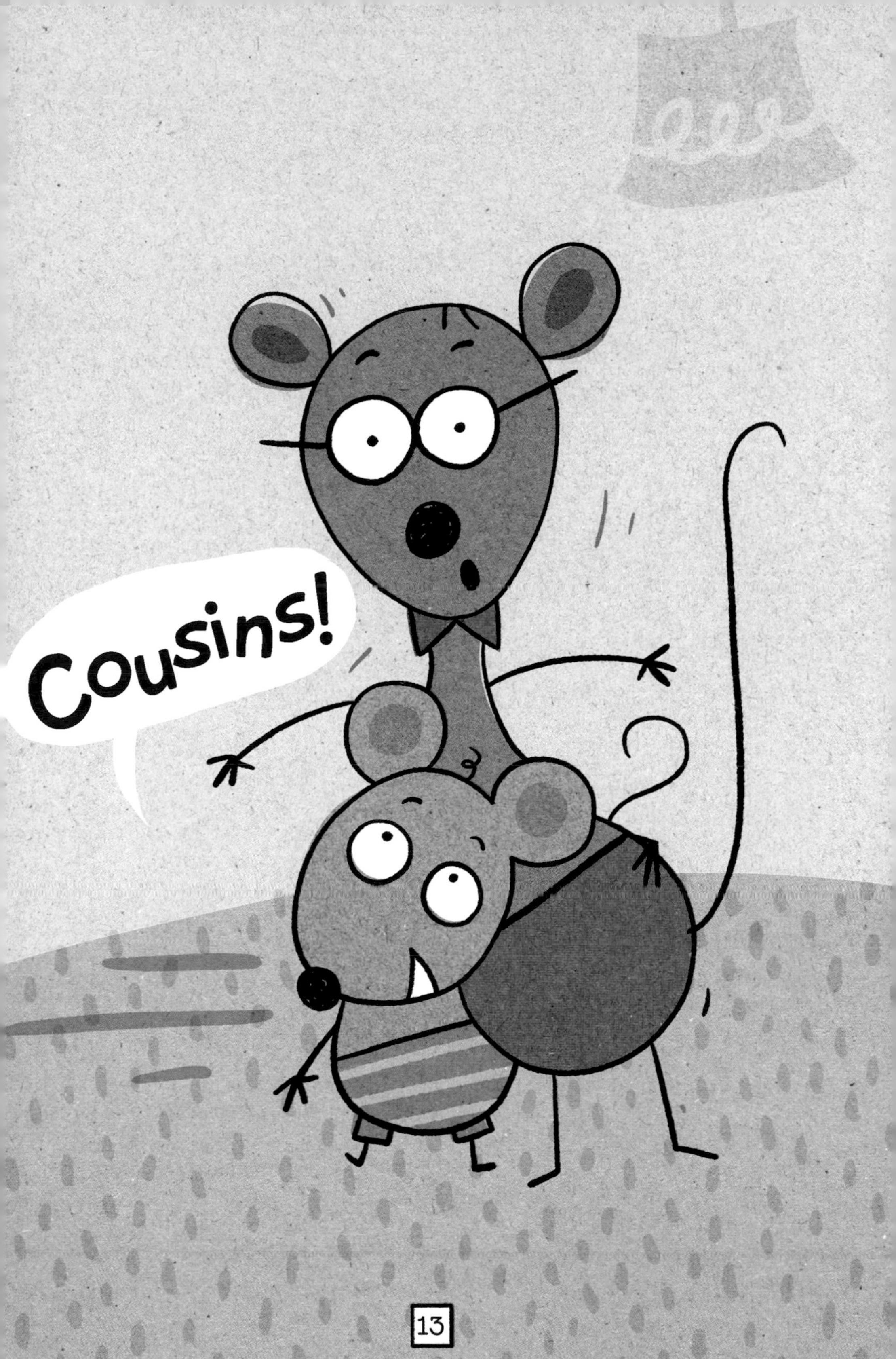
Cousins!

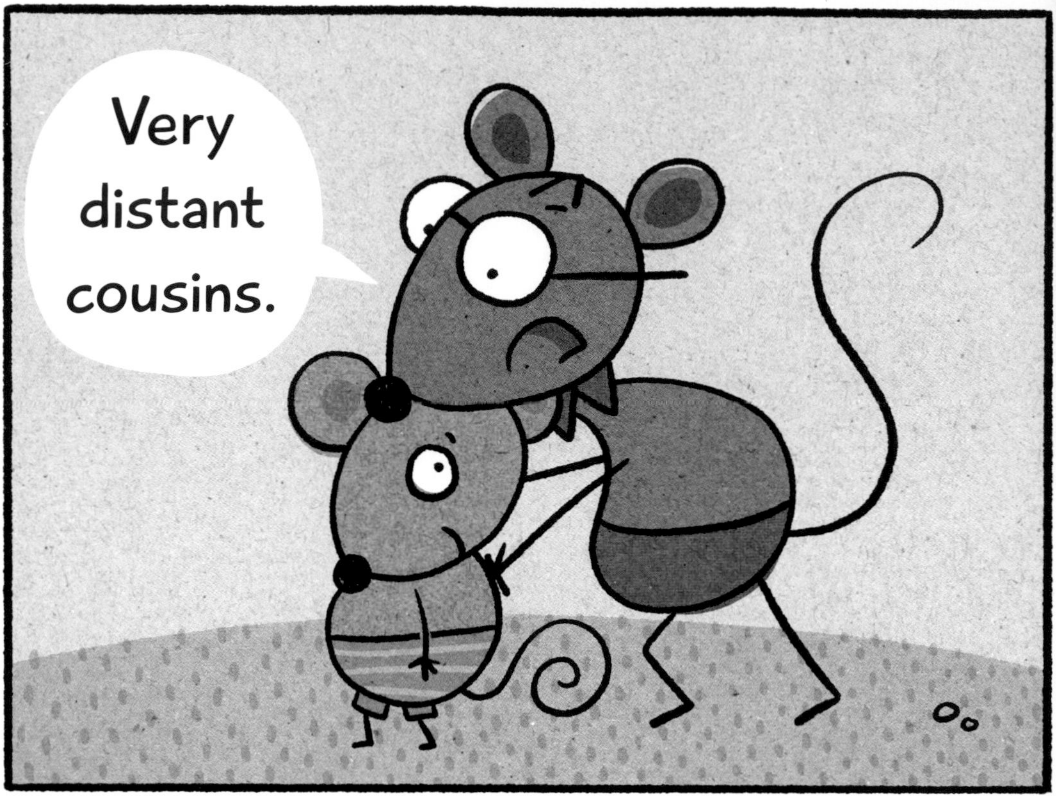
Very distant cousins.

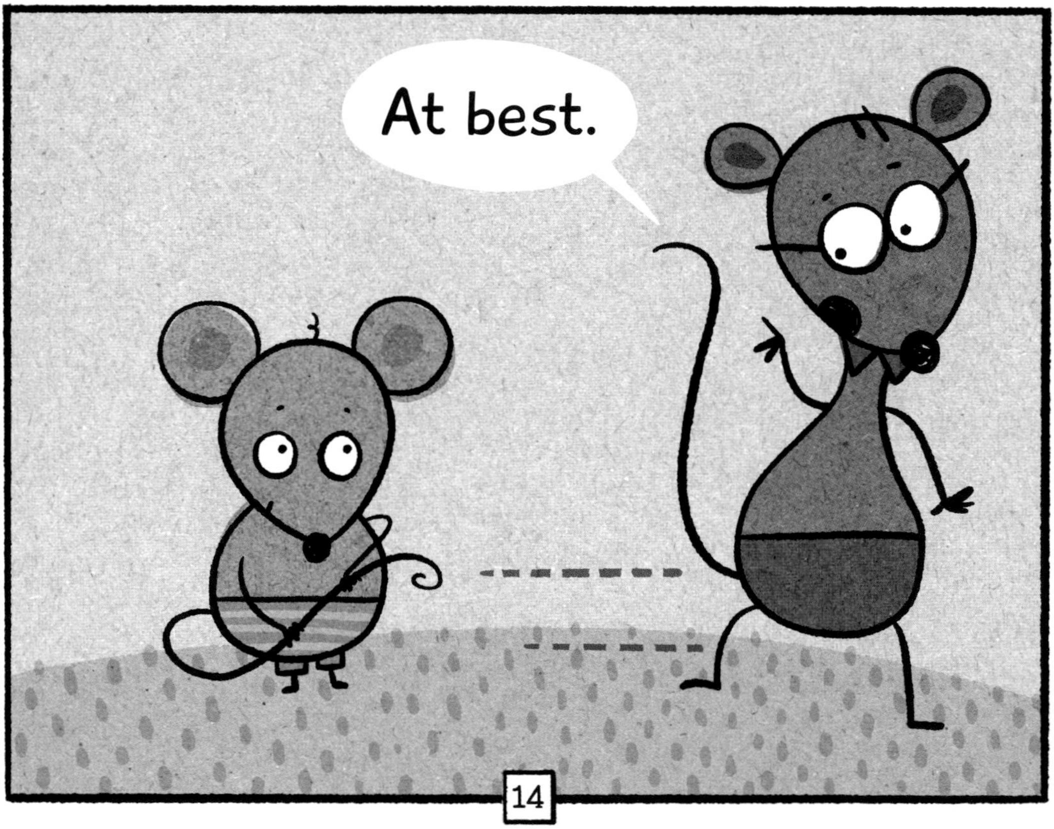
At best.

Gasp!

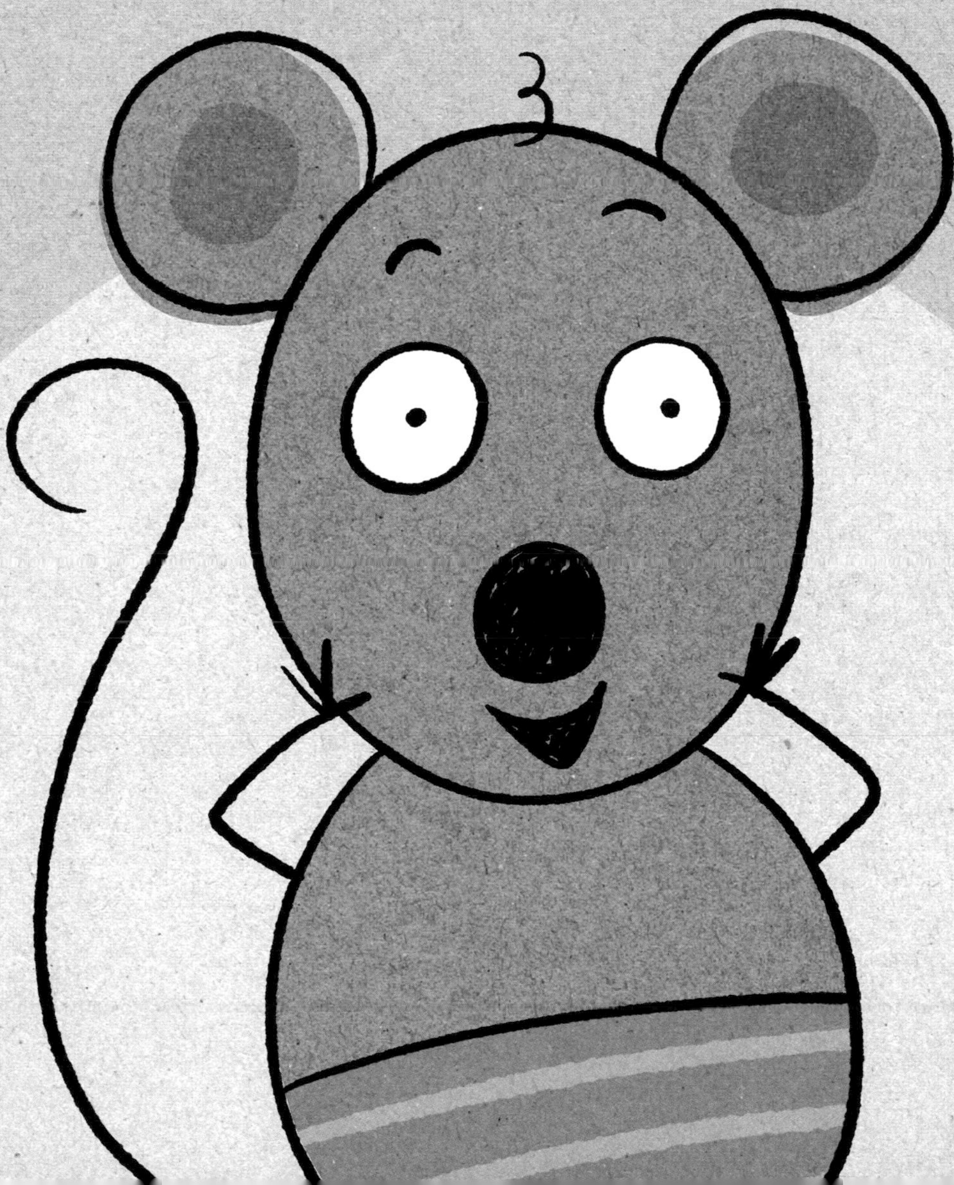

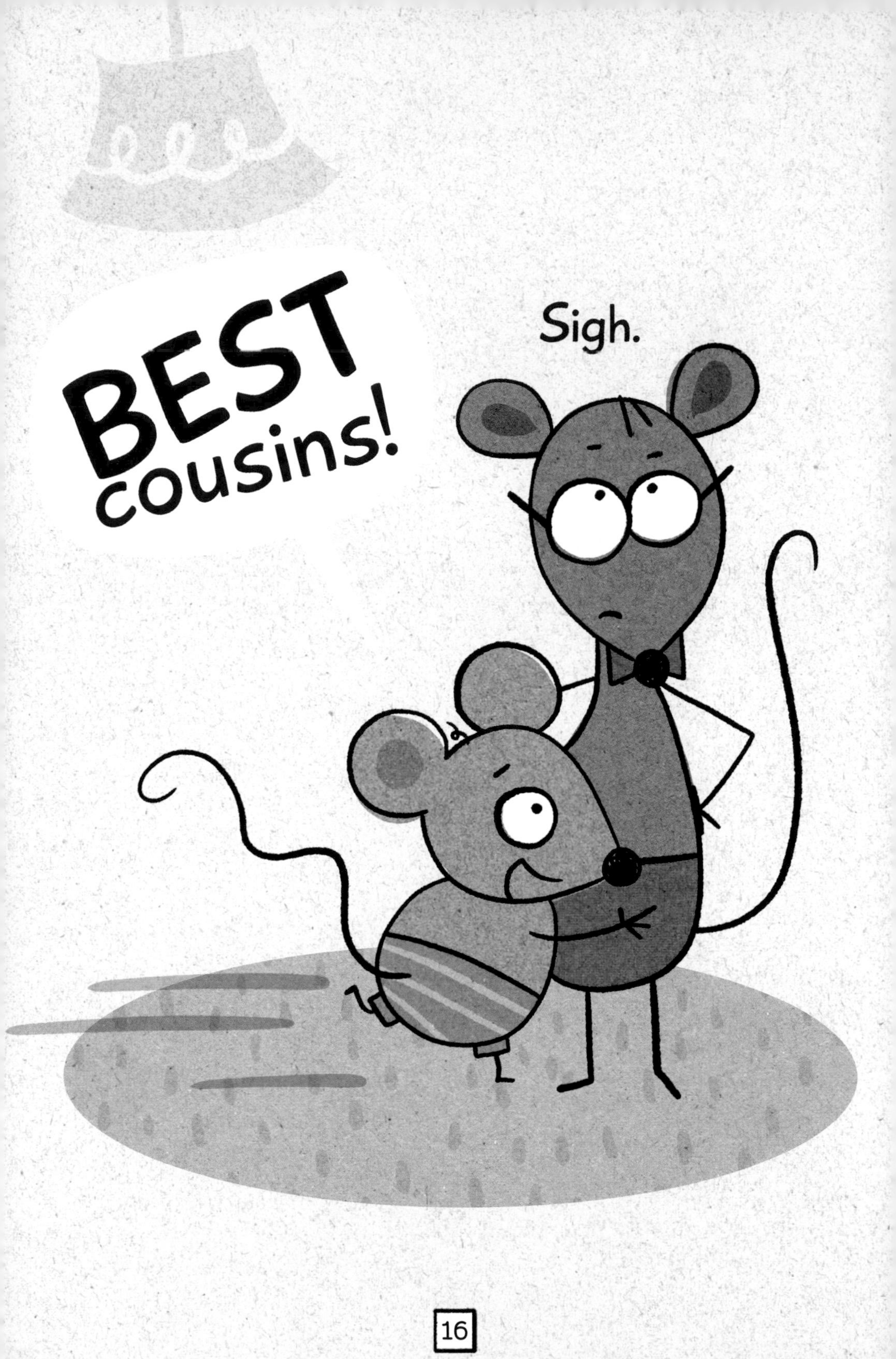
BEST cousins!
Sigh.

Boone's Guide to Common Rodents

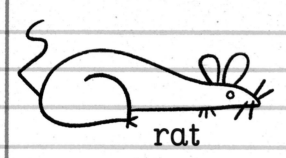

rat

mouse

hamster

gerbil

guinea
pig

Figgy's
Family Album

me

my brother
Boone

Chapter 2
Next Brother

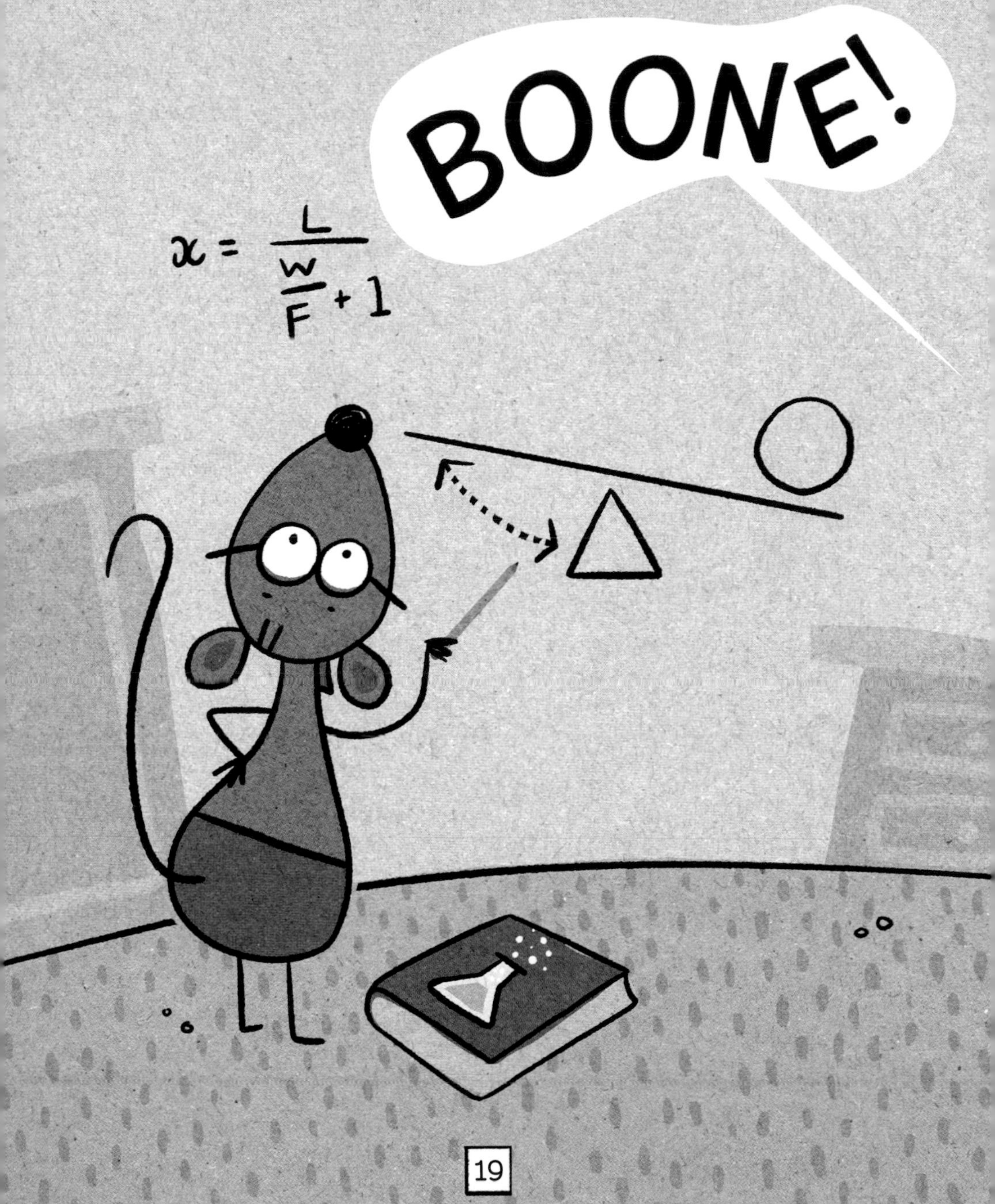
BOONE!
$x = \frac{L}{\frac{W}{F} + 1}$

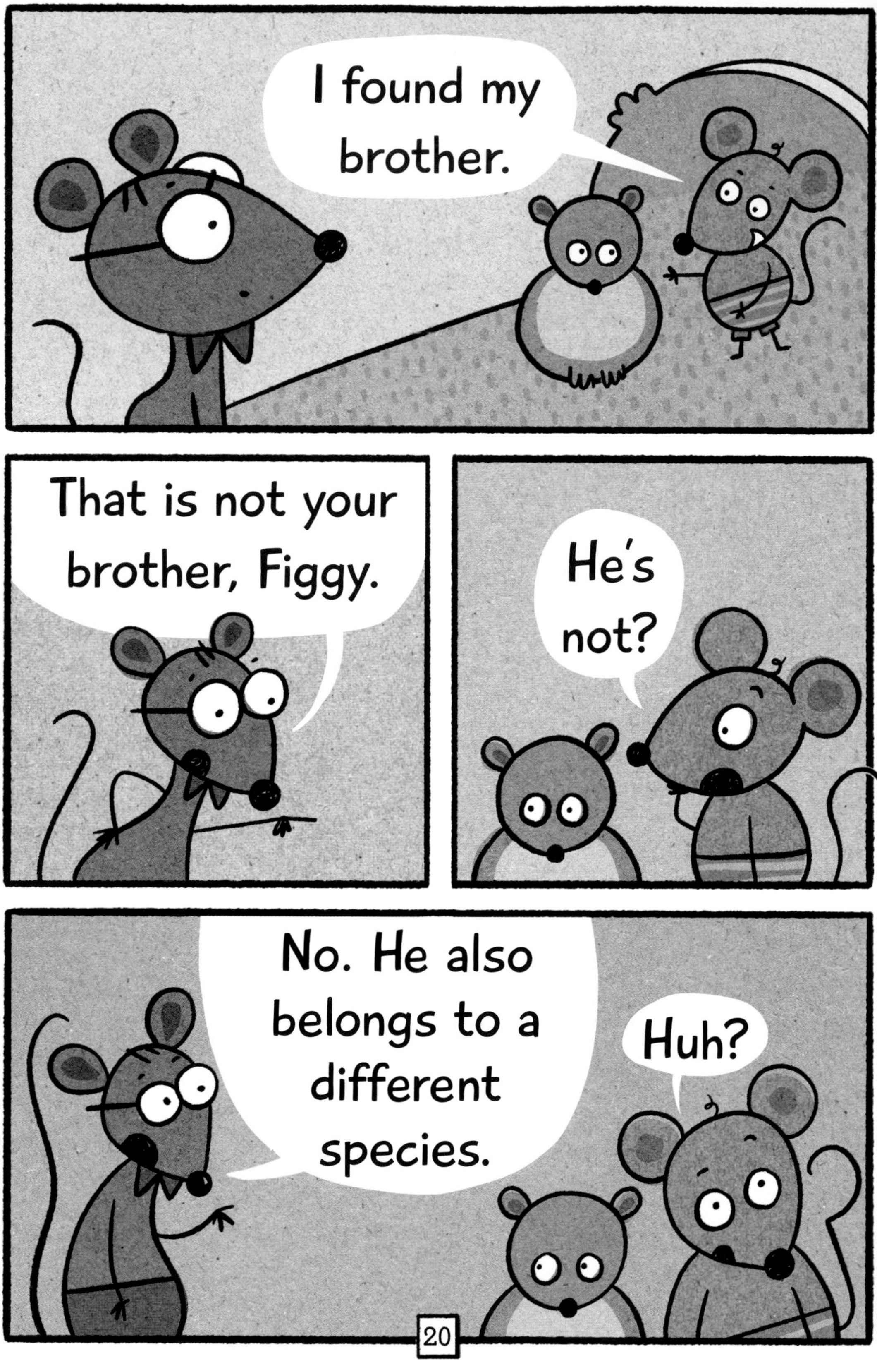
I found my brother.
That is not your brother, Figgy.
He's not?
No. He also belongs to a different species.
Huh?

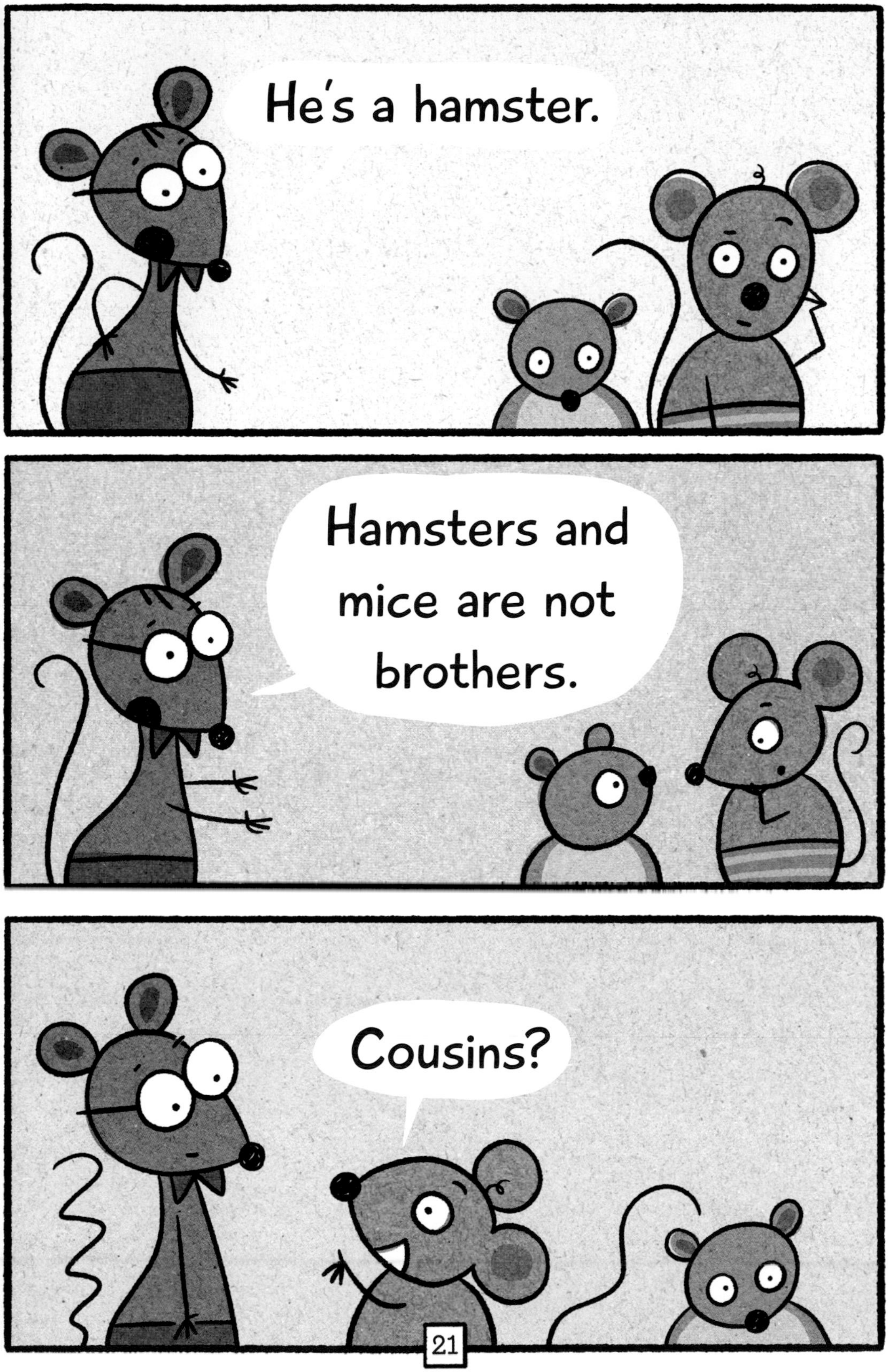
He's a hamster.
Hamsters and mice are not brothers.
Cousins?

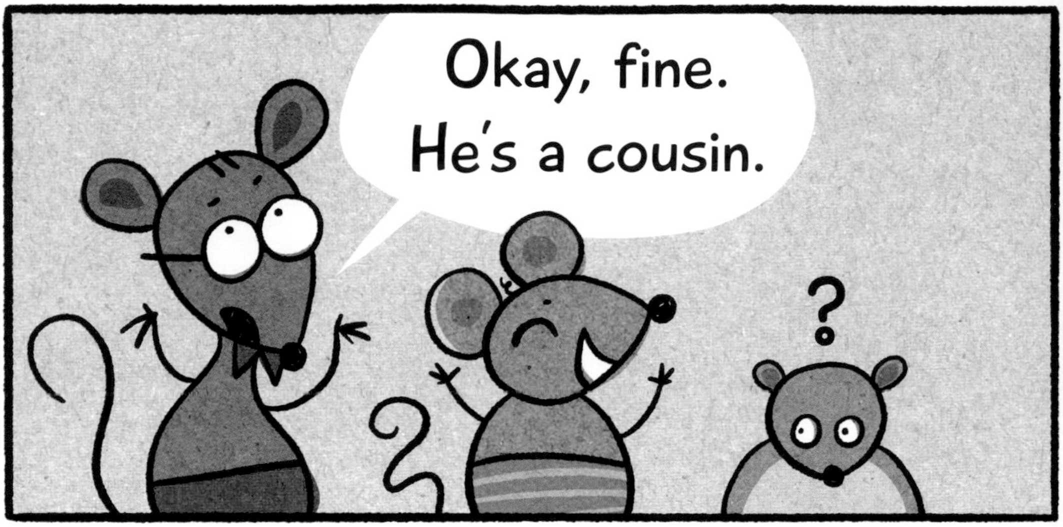
Okay, fine.
He's a cousin.
?

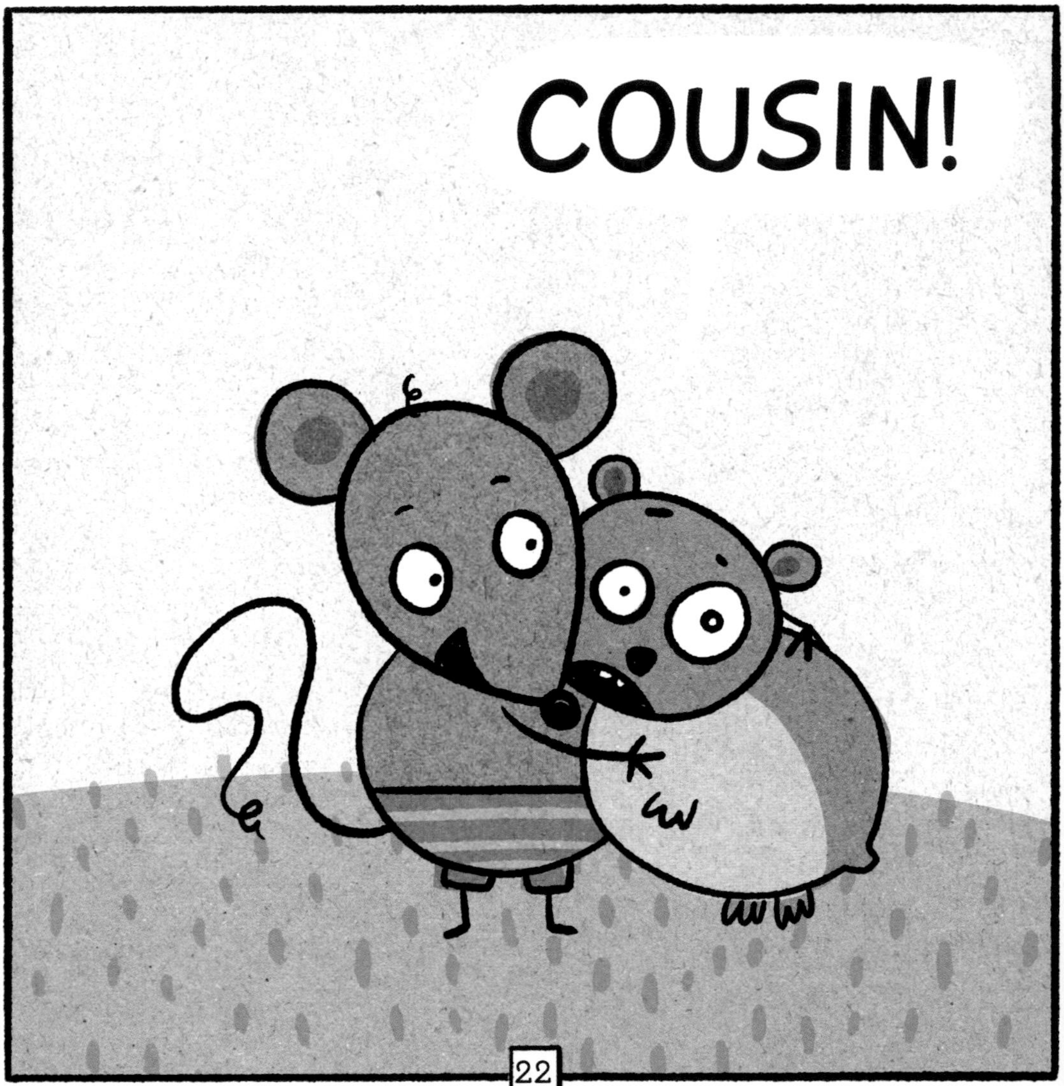
COUSIN!

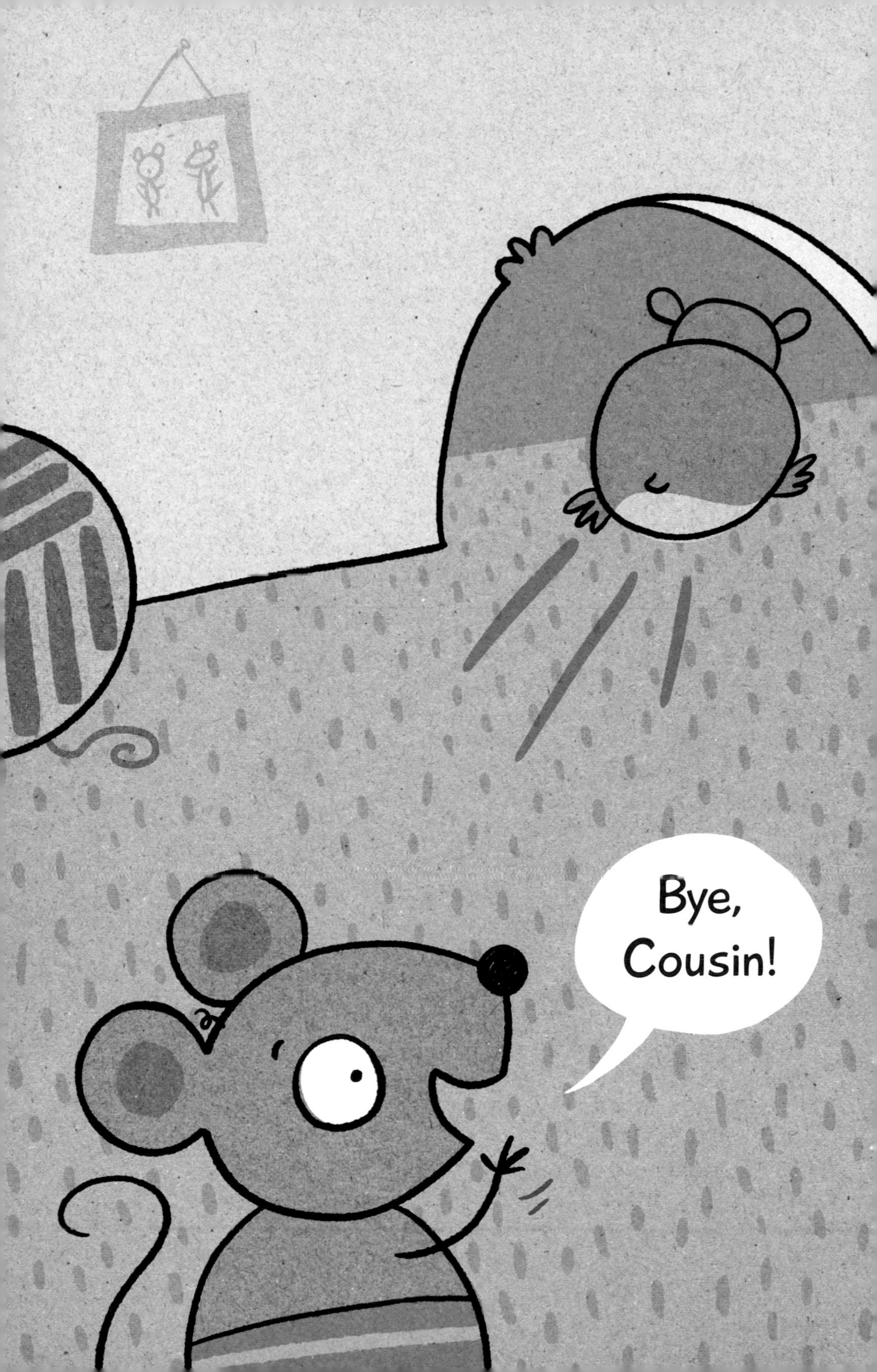
Bye, Cousin!

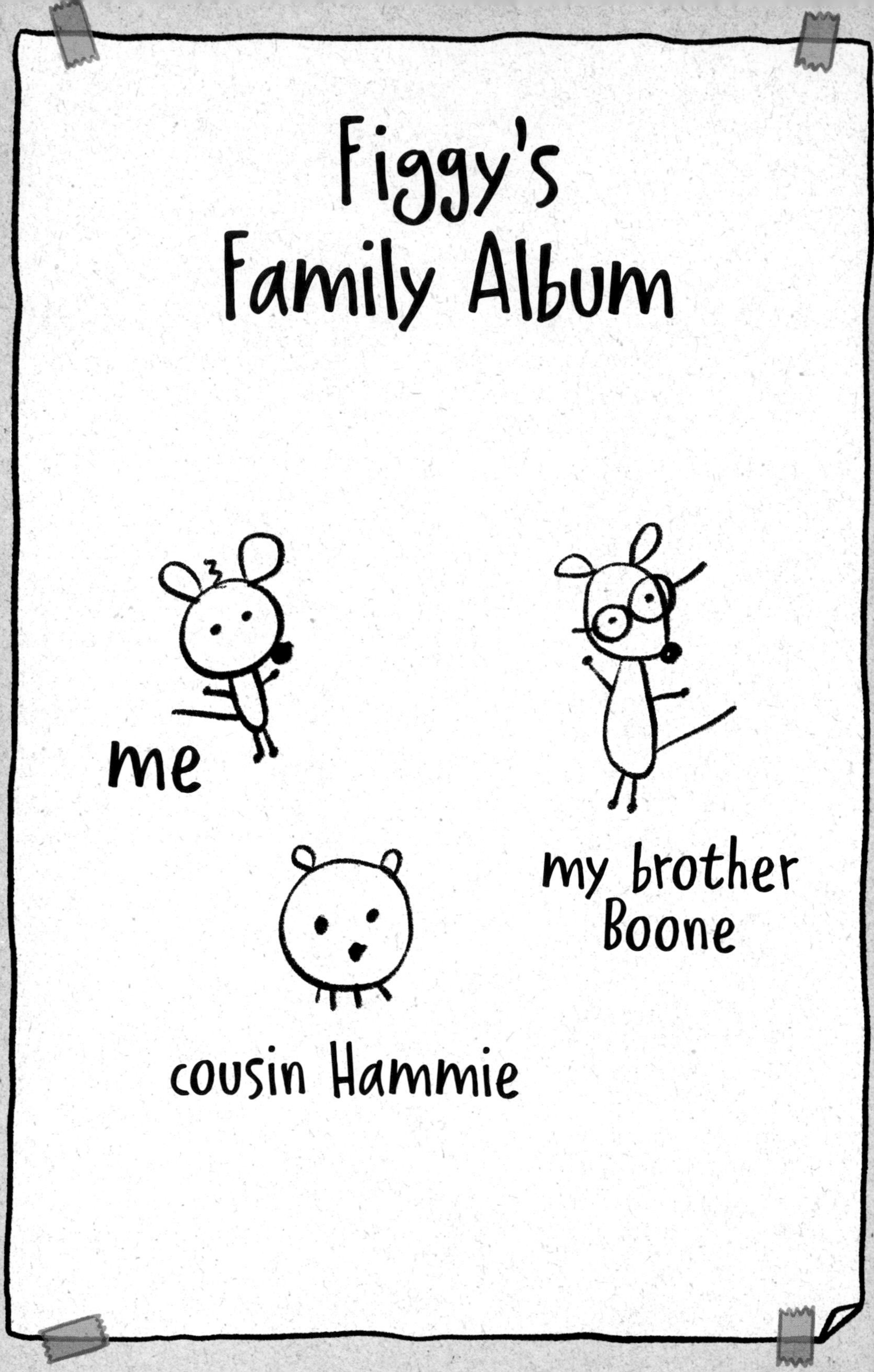
Figgy's
Family Album
me
my brother
Boone
cousin Hammie

$$x = \frac{L}{\frac{W}{F}+1}$$

BOONE!

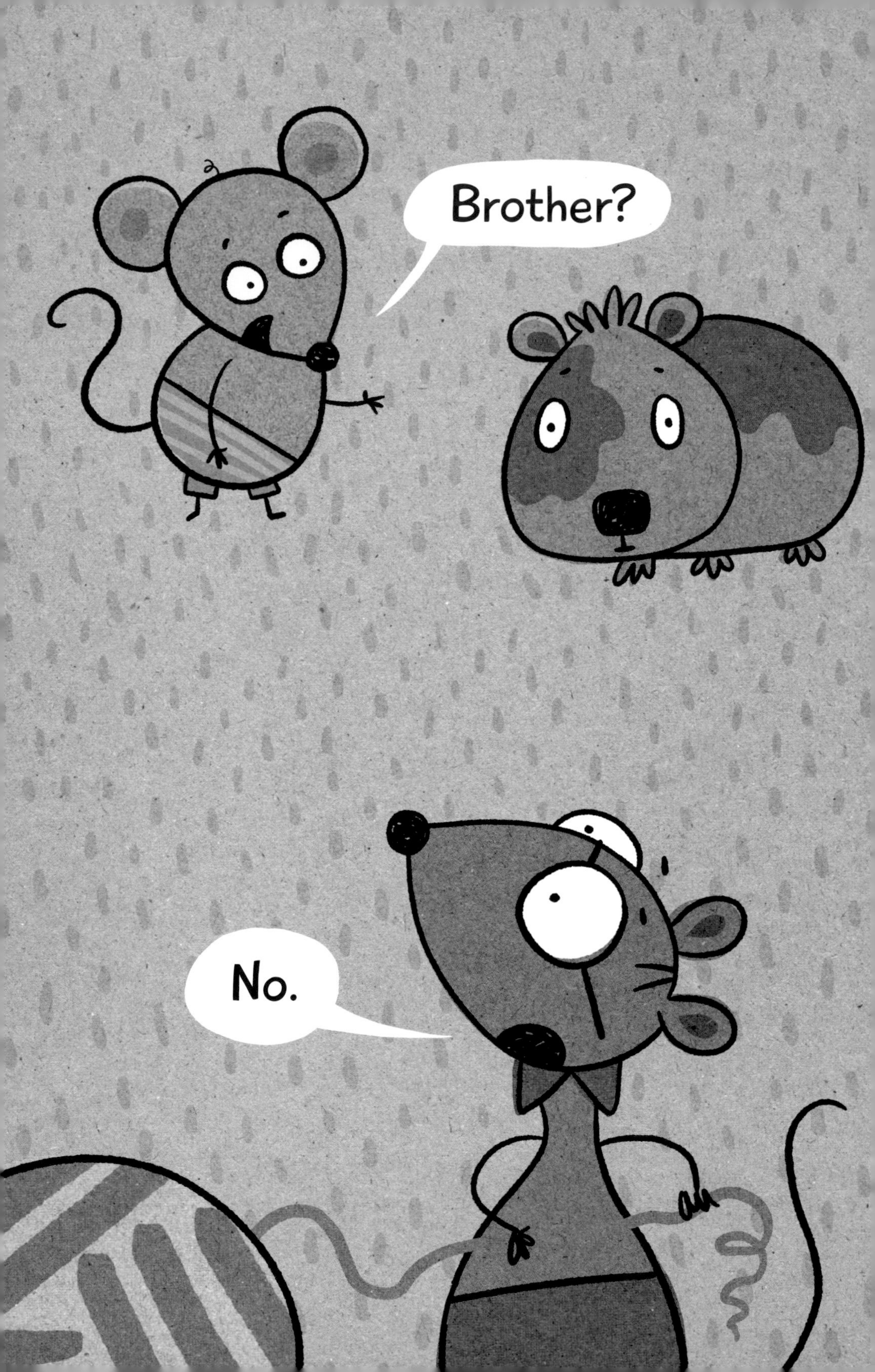
Brother?
No.

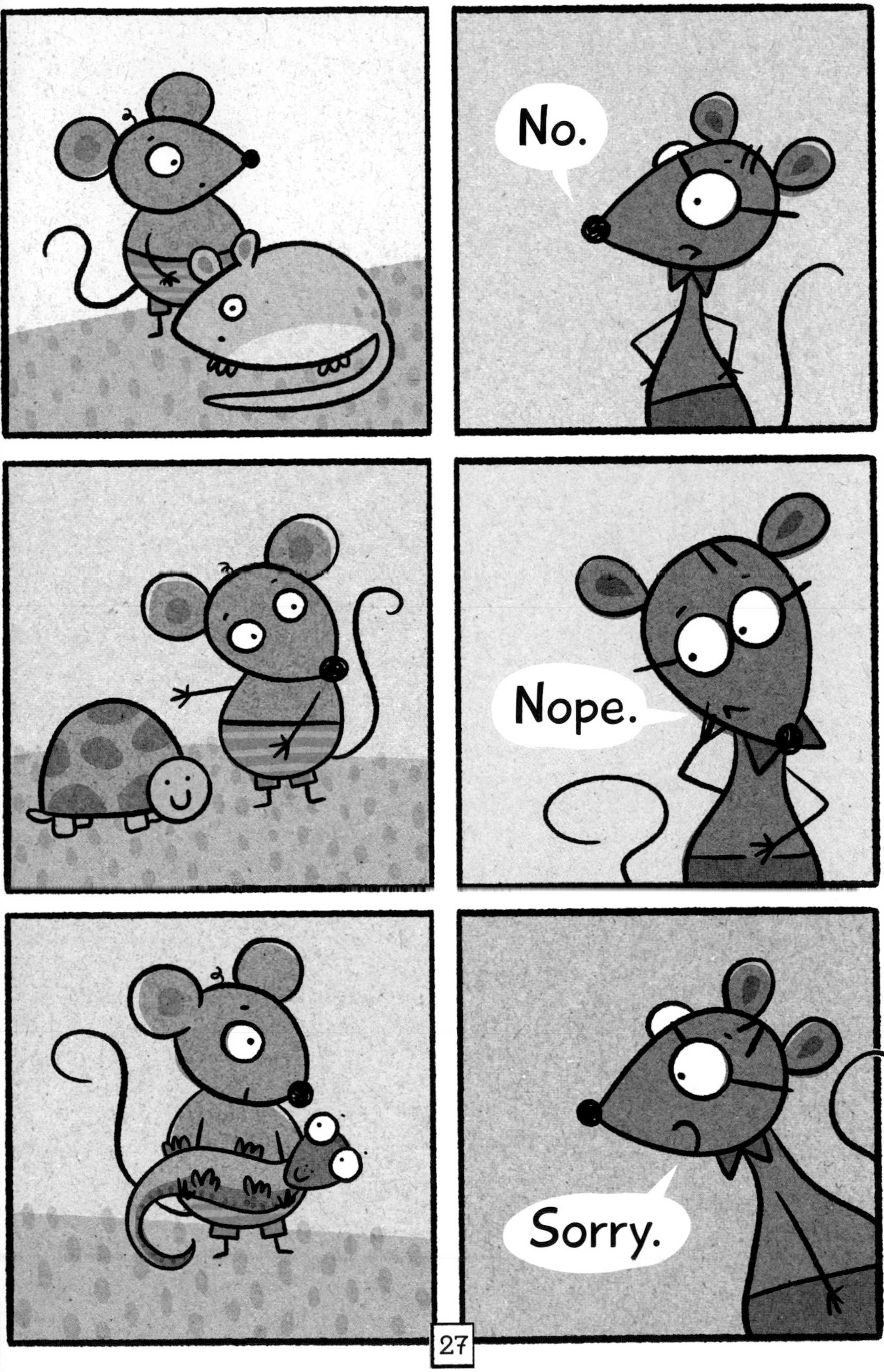
No.
Nope.
Sorry.

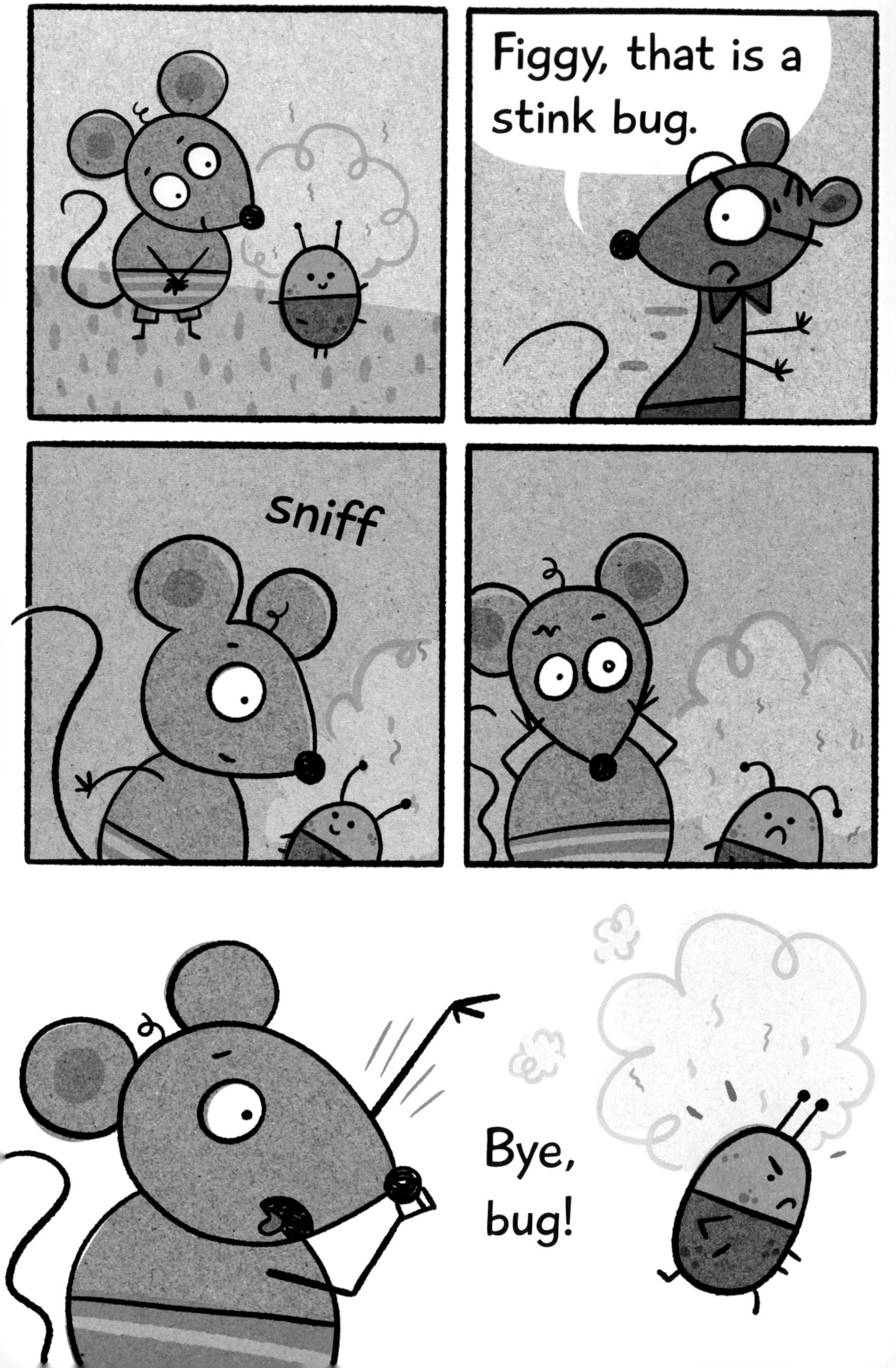
Figgy, that is a stink bug.
sniff
Bye, bug!

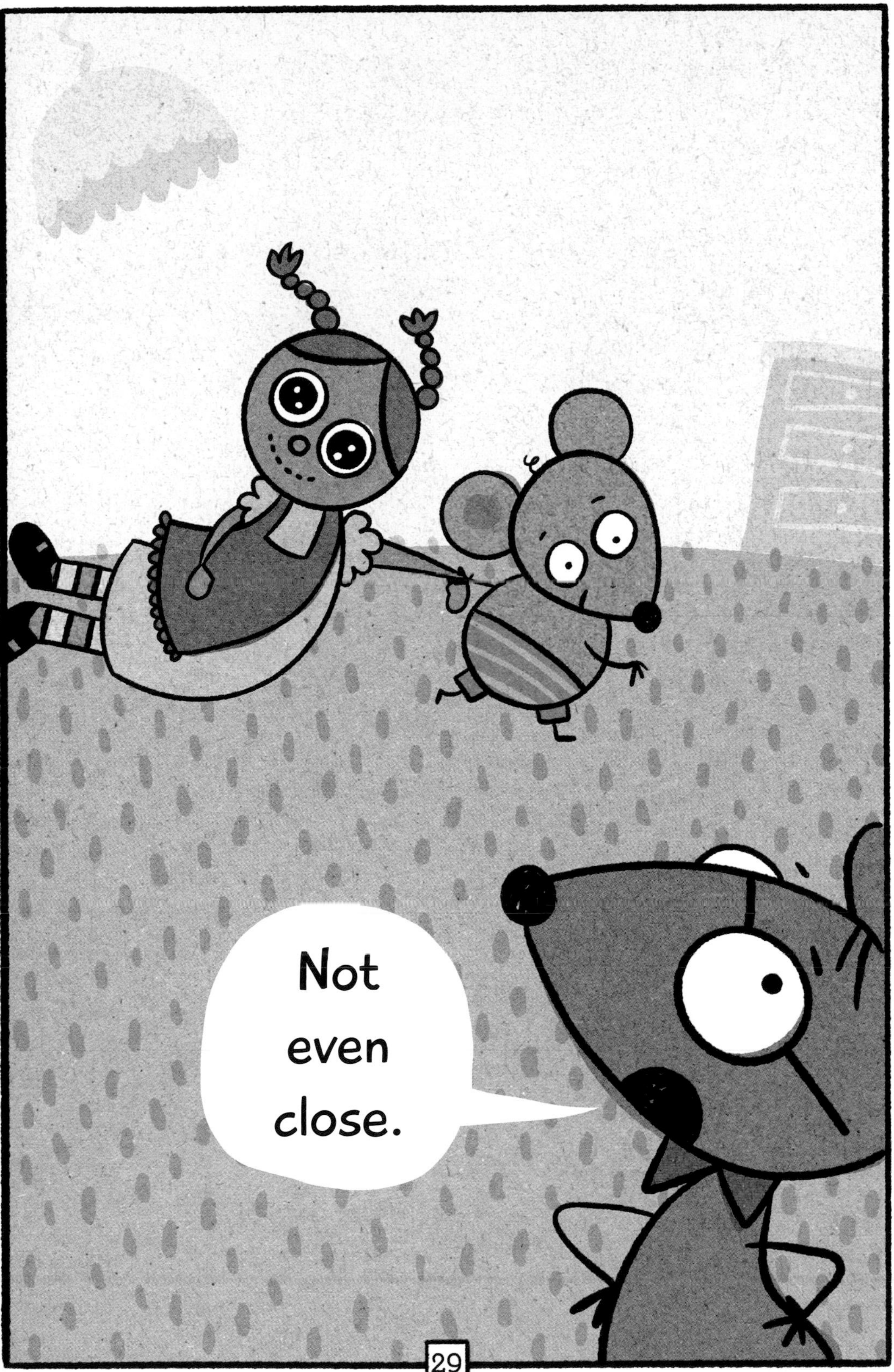
Not even close.

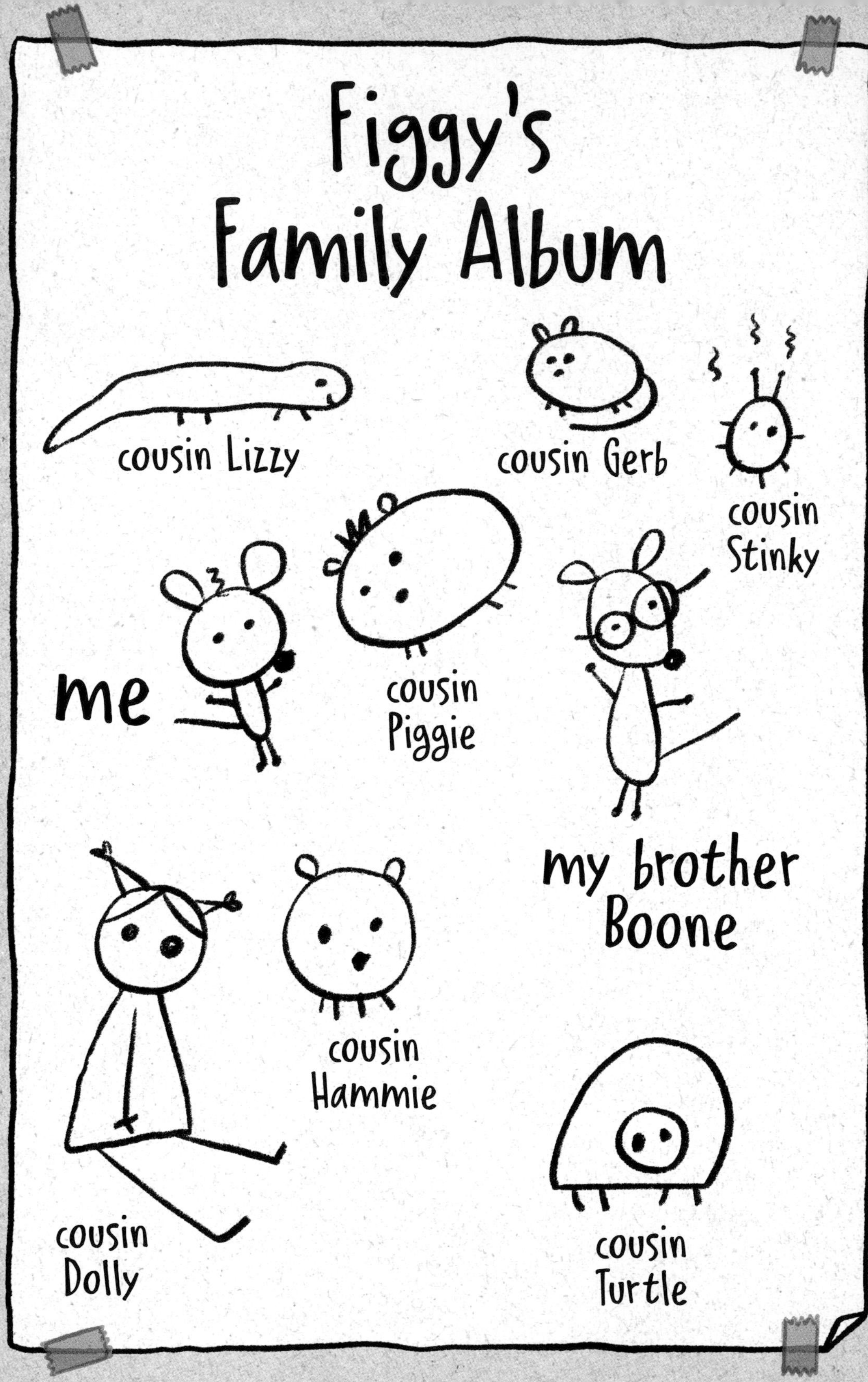
Figgy's Family Album
cousin Lizzy
cousin Gerb
cousin Stinky
me
cousin Piggie
my brother Boone
cousin Hammie
cousin Dolly
cousin Turtle

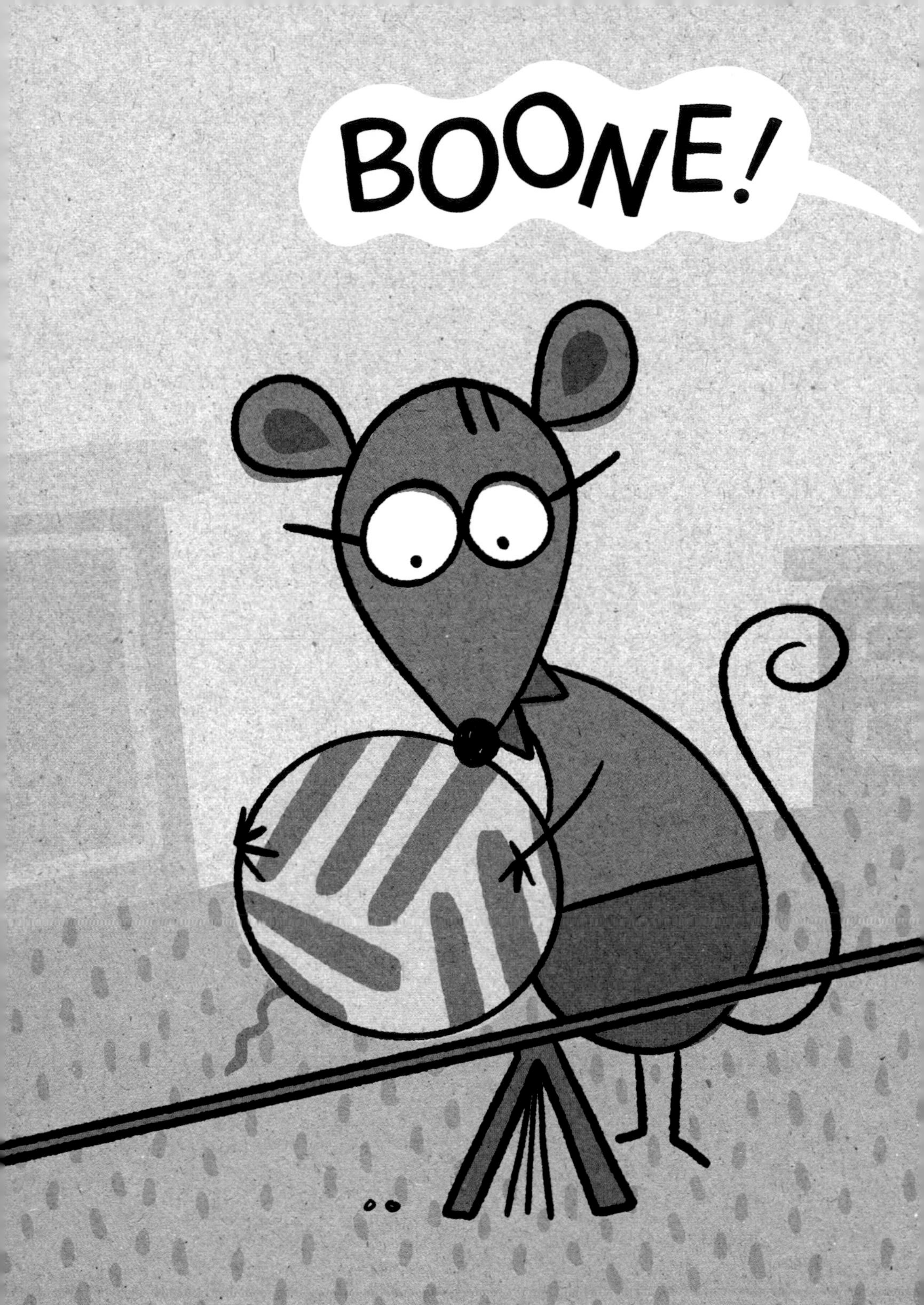
BOONE!

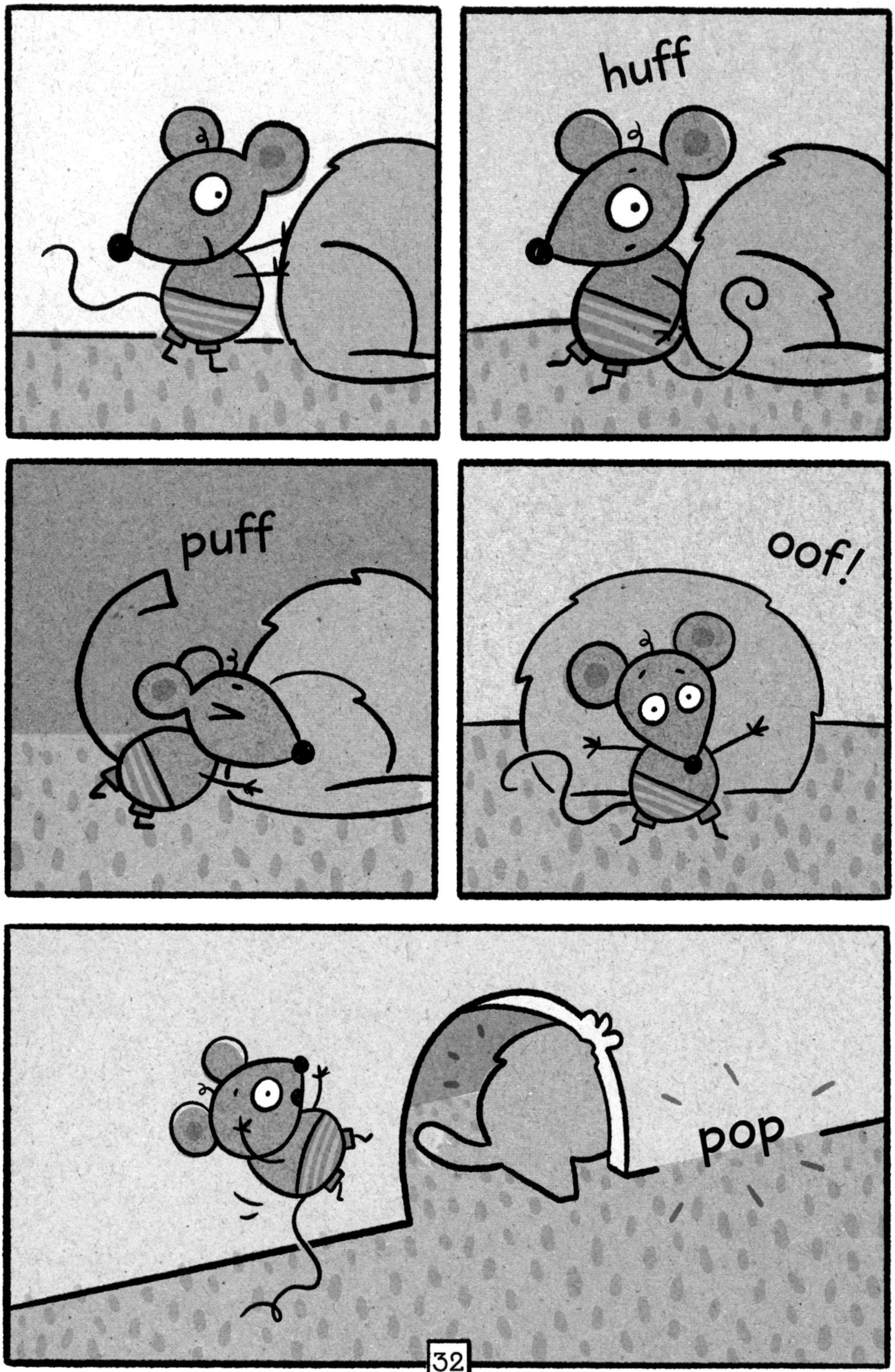
huff
puff
oof!
pop

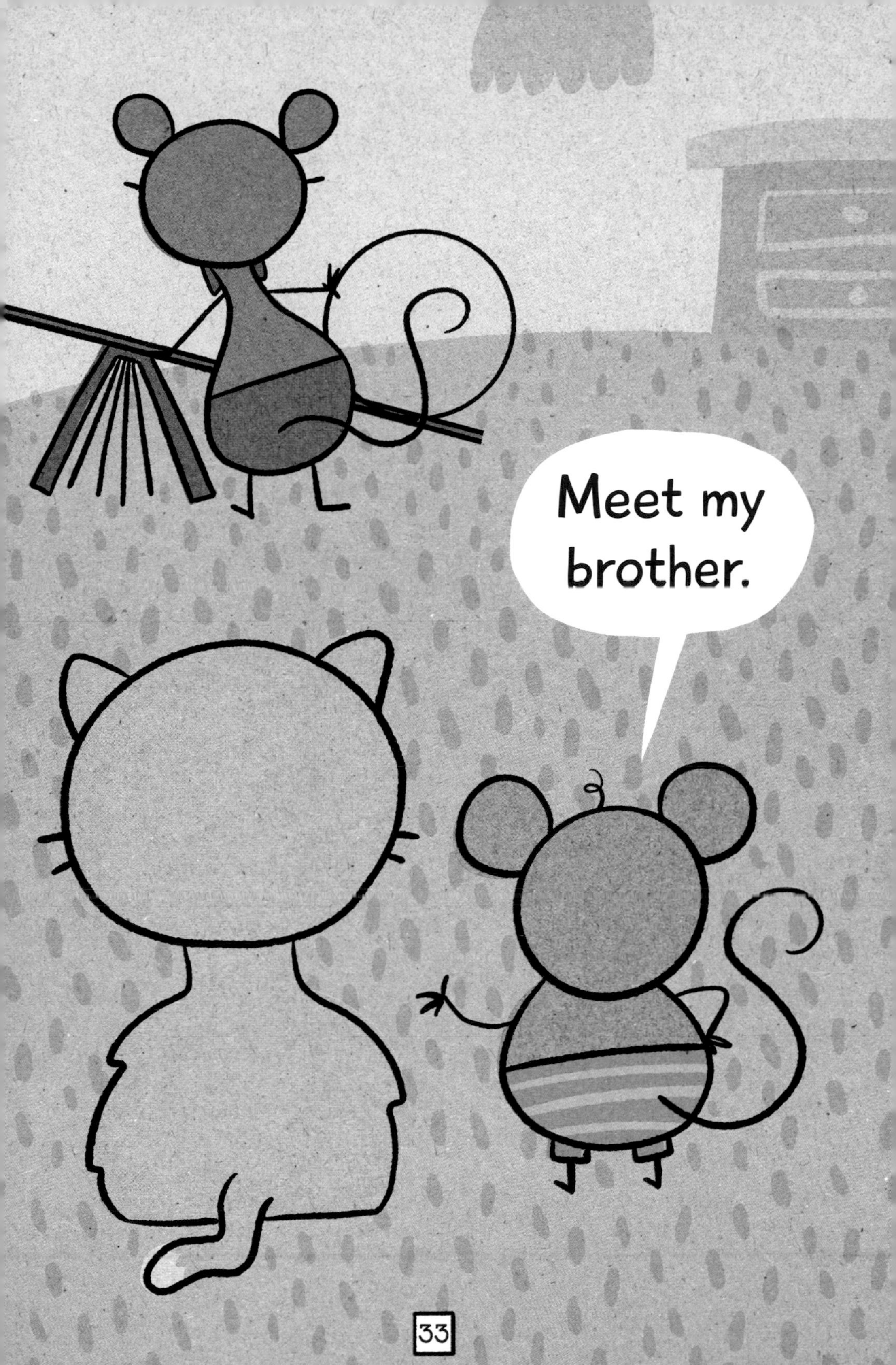
Meet my brother.

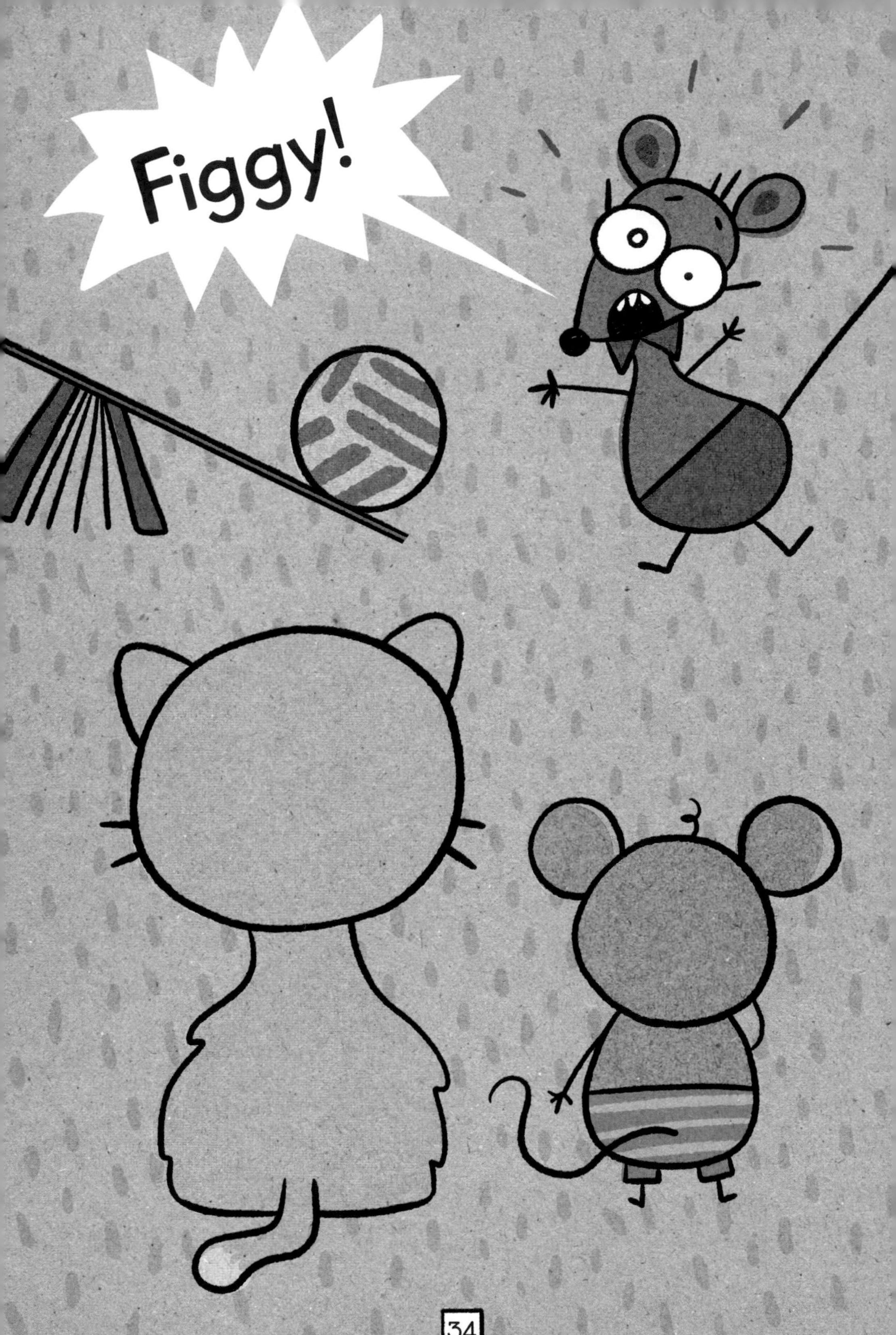
Figgy!

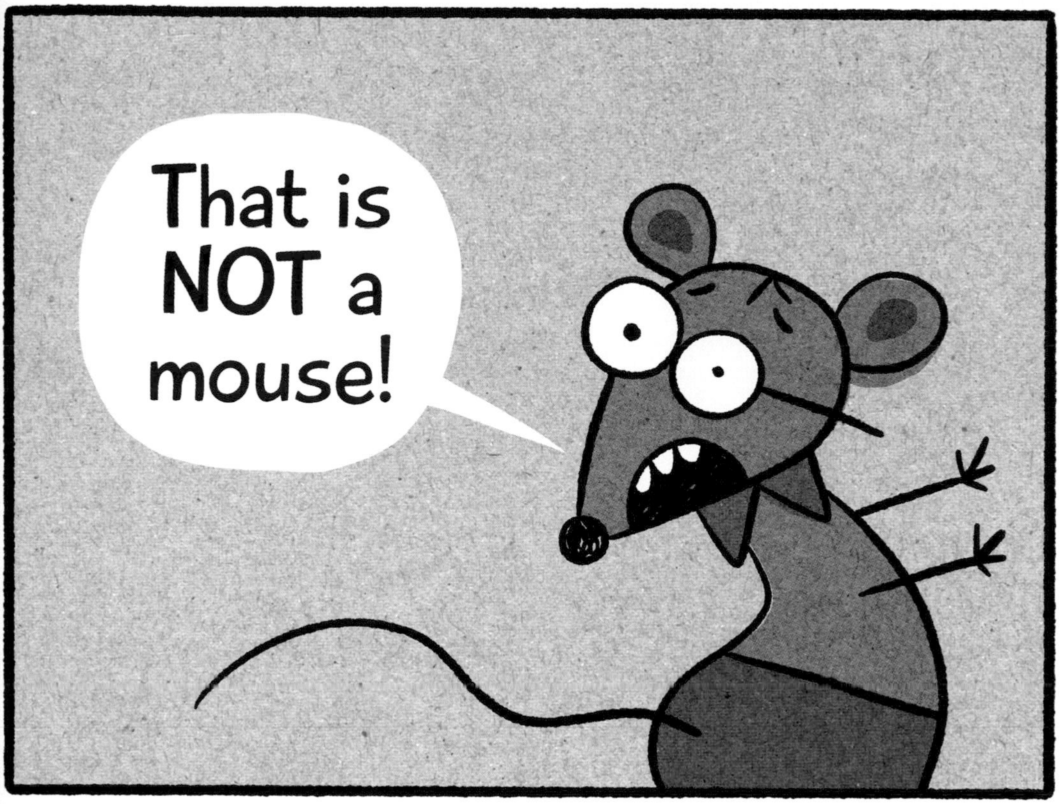
That is NOT a mouse!

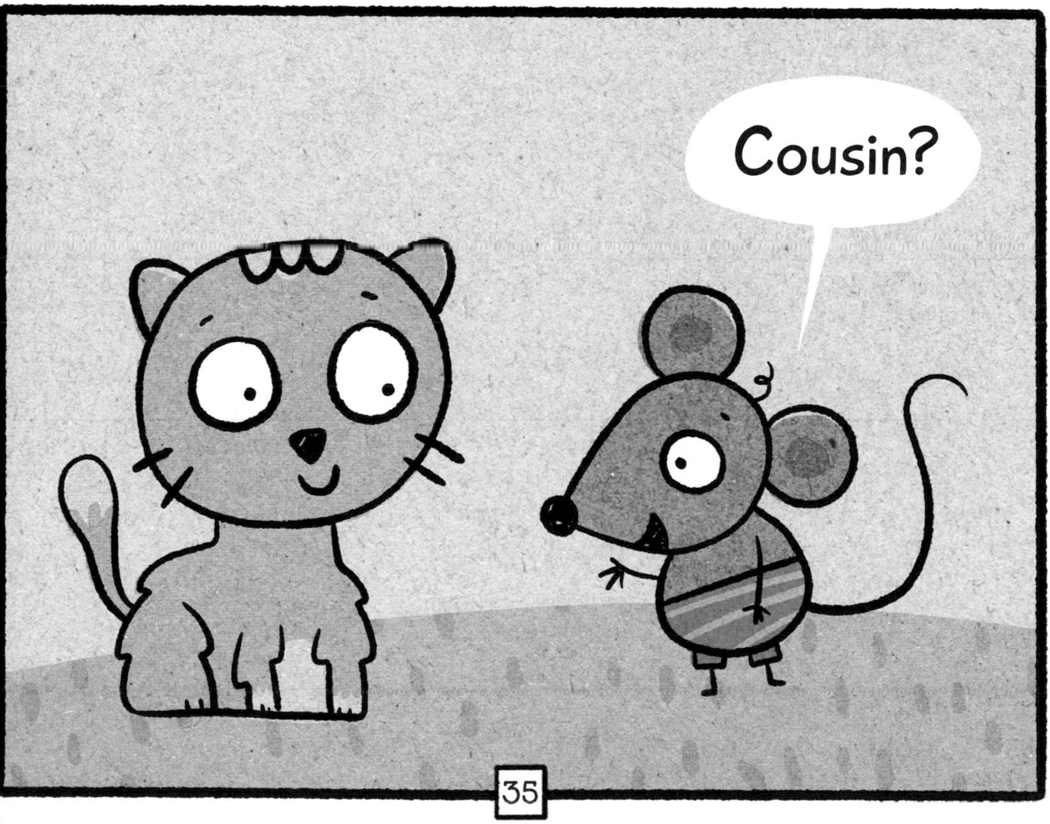
Cousin?

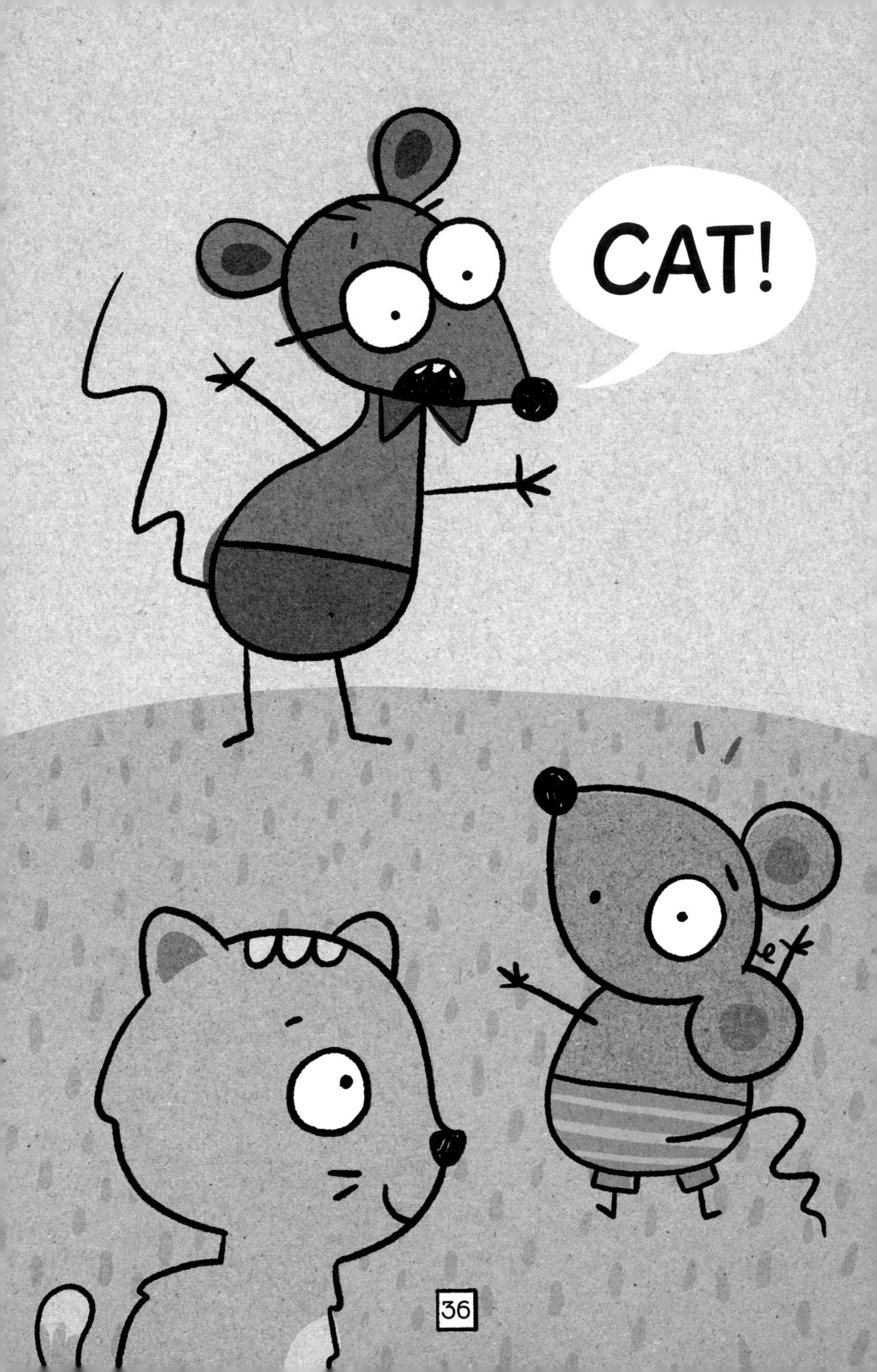
CAT!

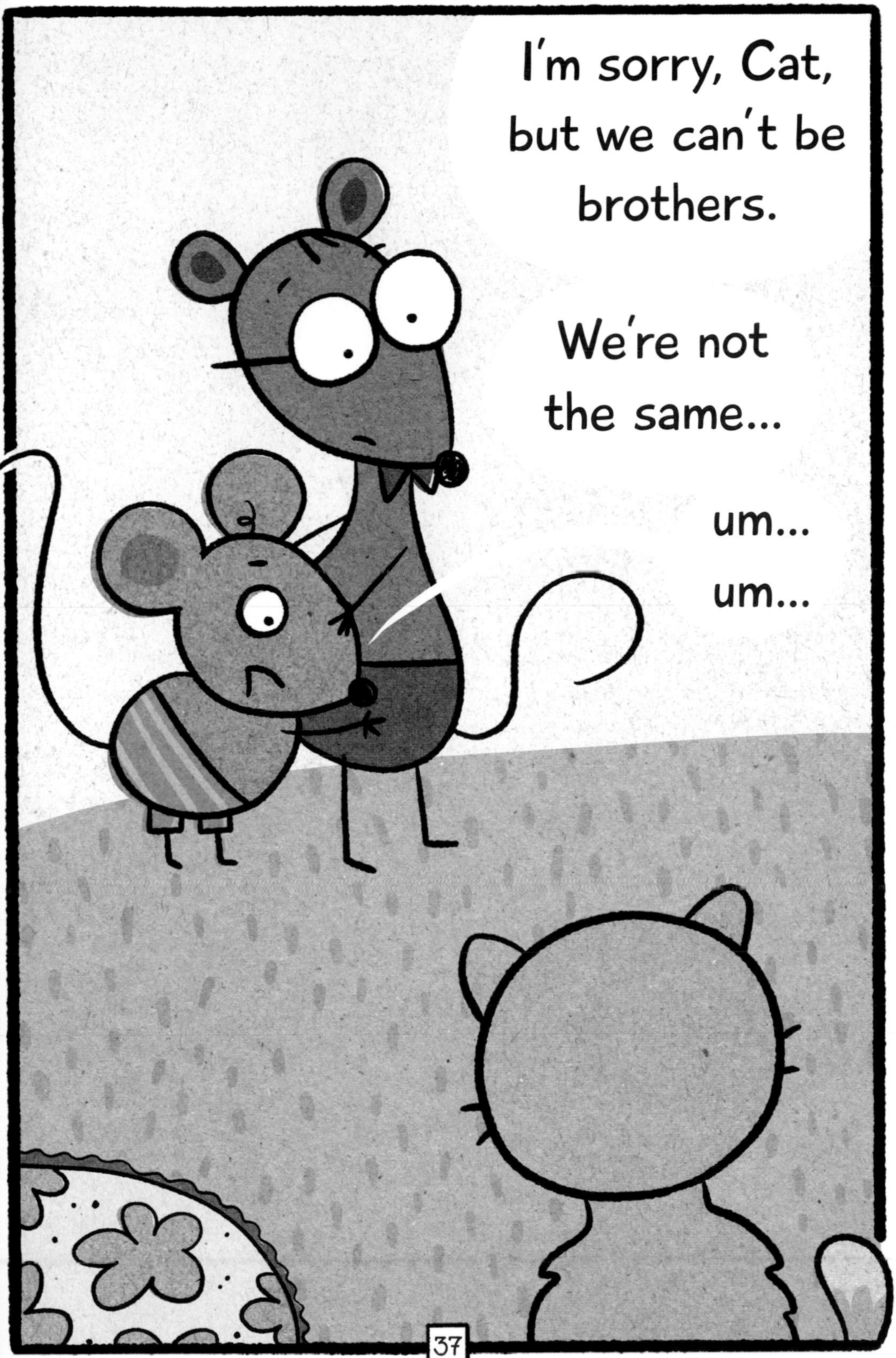
I'm sorry, Cat, but we can't be brothers.
We're not the same...
um...
um...

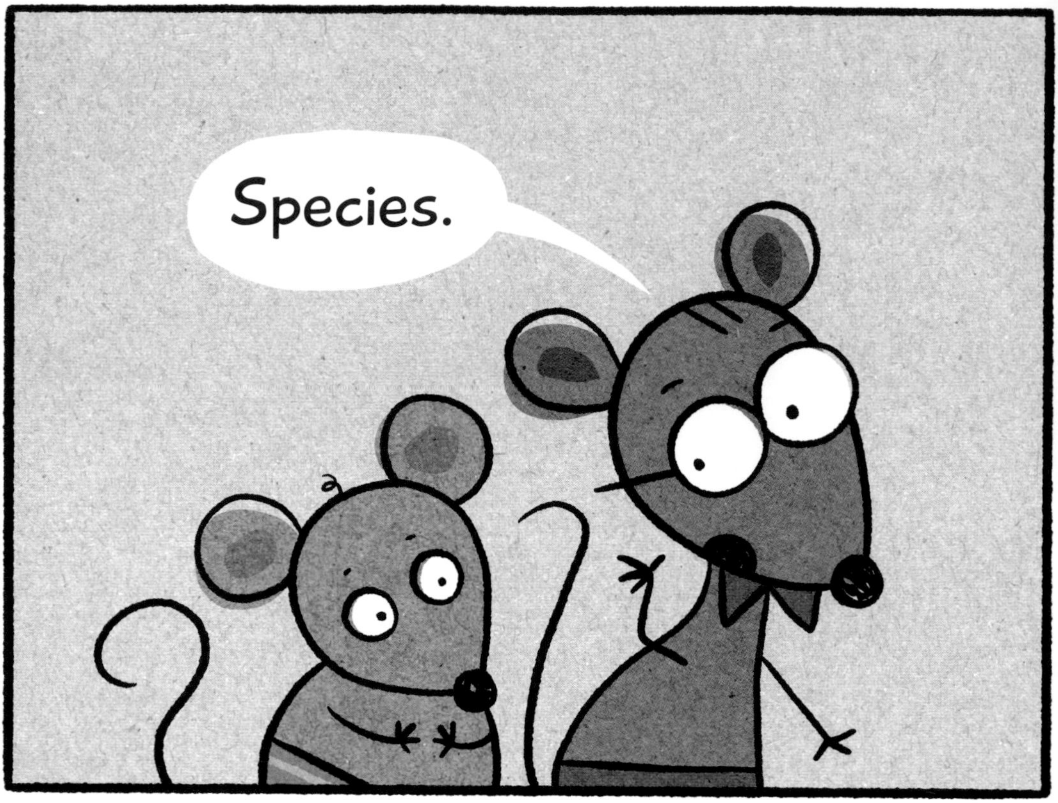
Species.

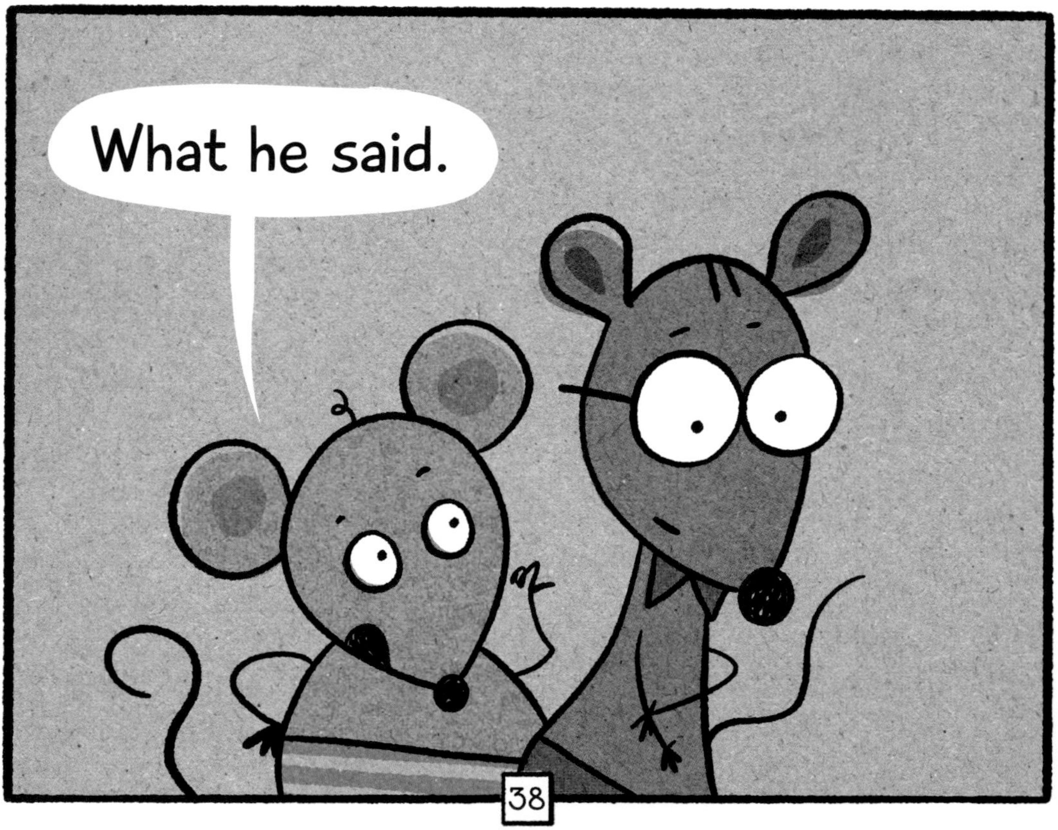
What he said.

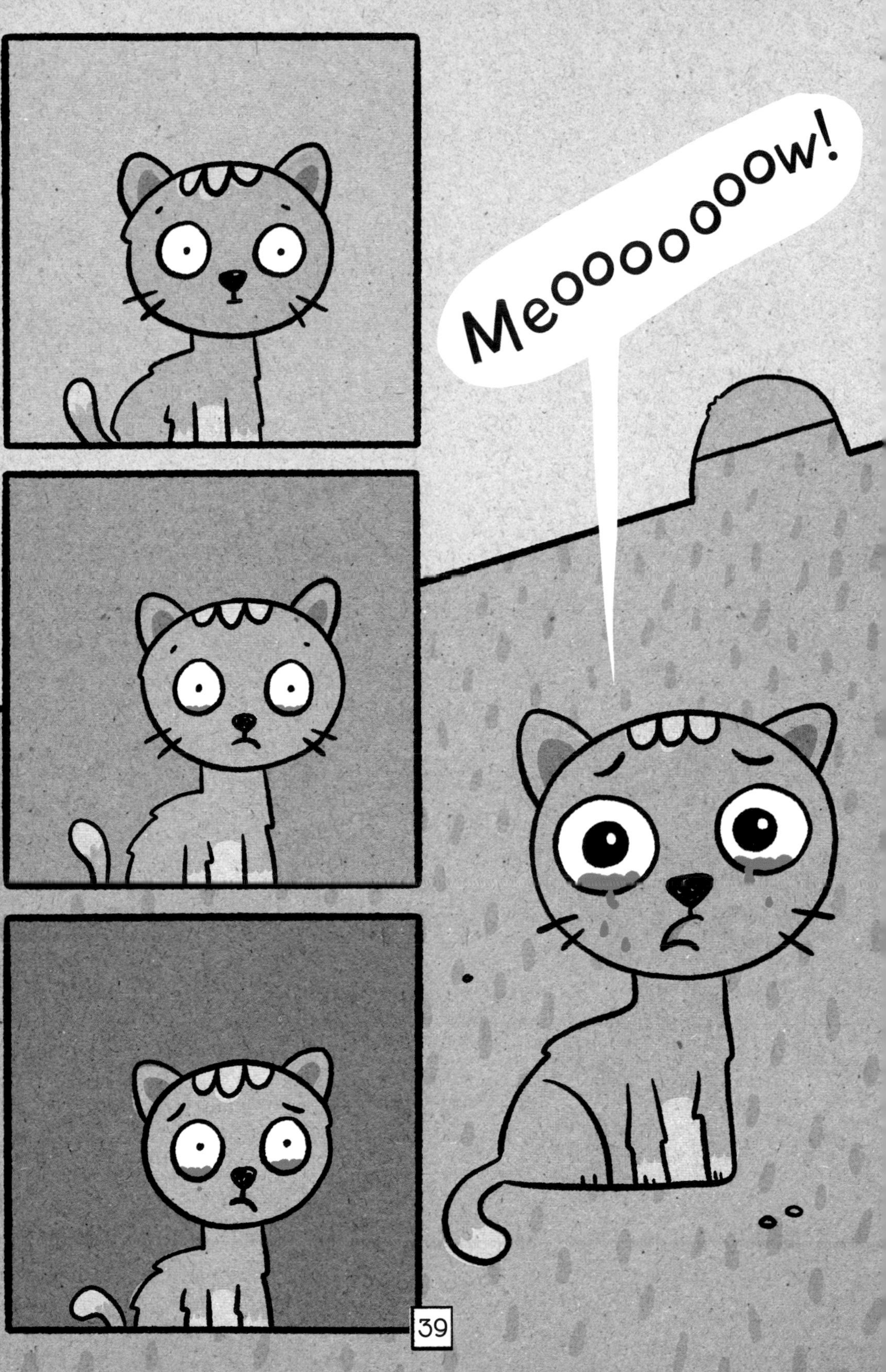
Meoooooooow!

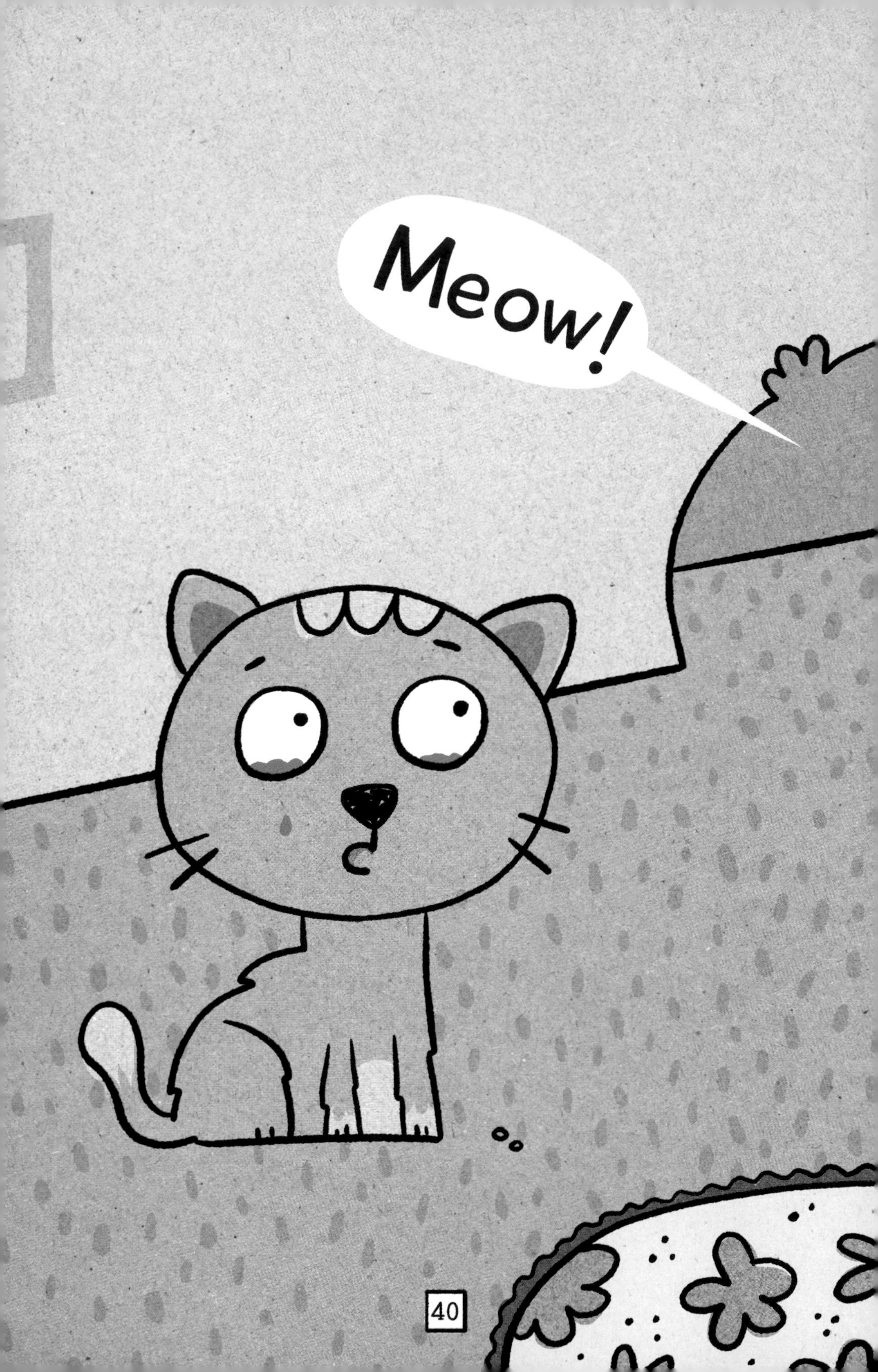
Meow!

Boone's Guide to the Food Chain

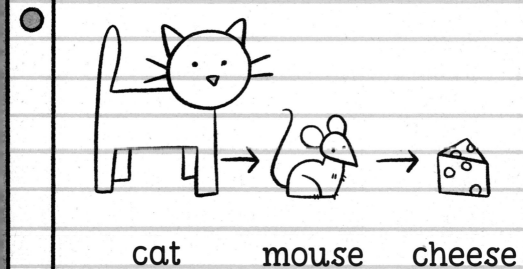

cat   mouse   cheese

Figgy's Favorite Foods

cheese

cheesy puff

cheesy noodles

cheesy toast

cheesy crackers

cheese pizza

cheesecake

Chapter 3
Oh Brother

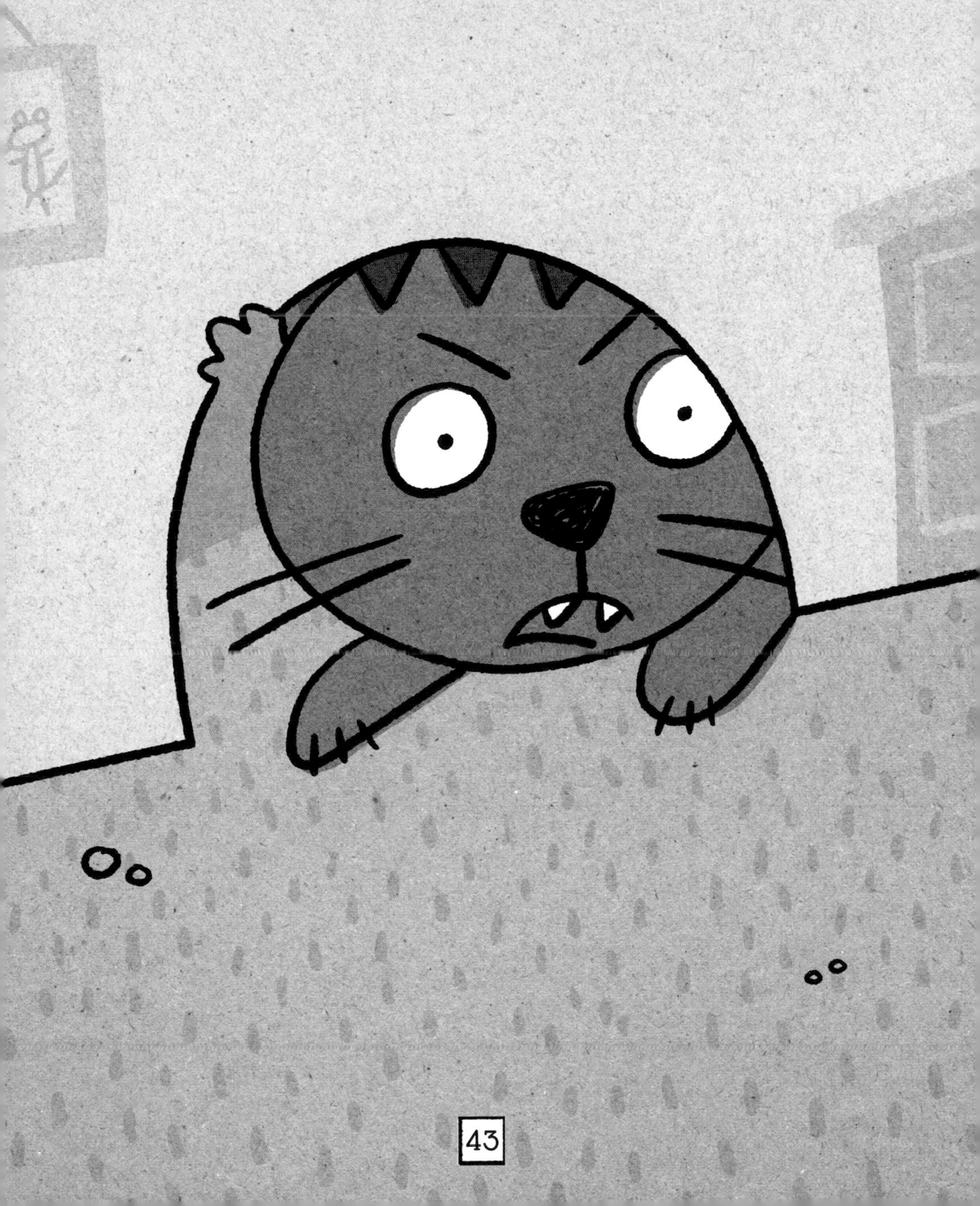

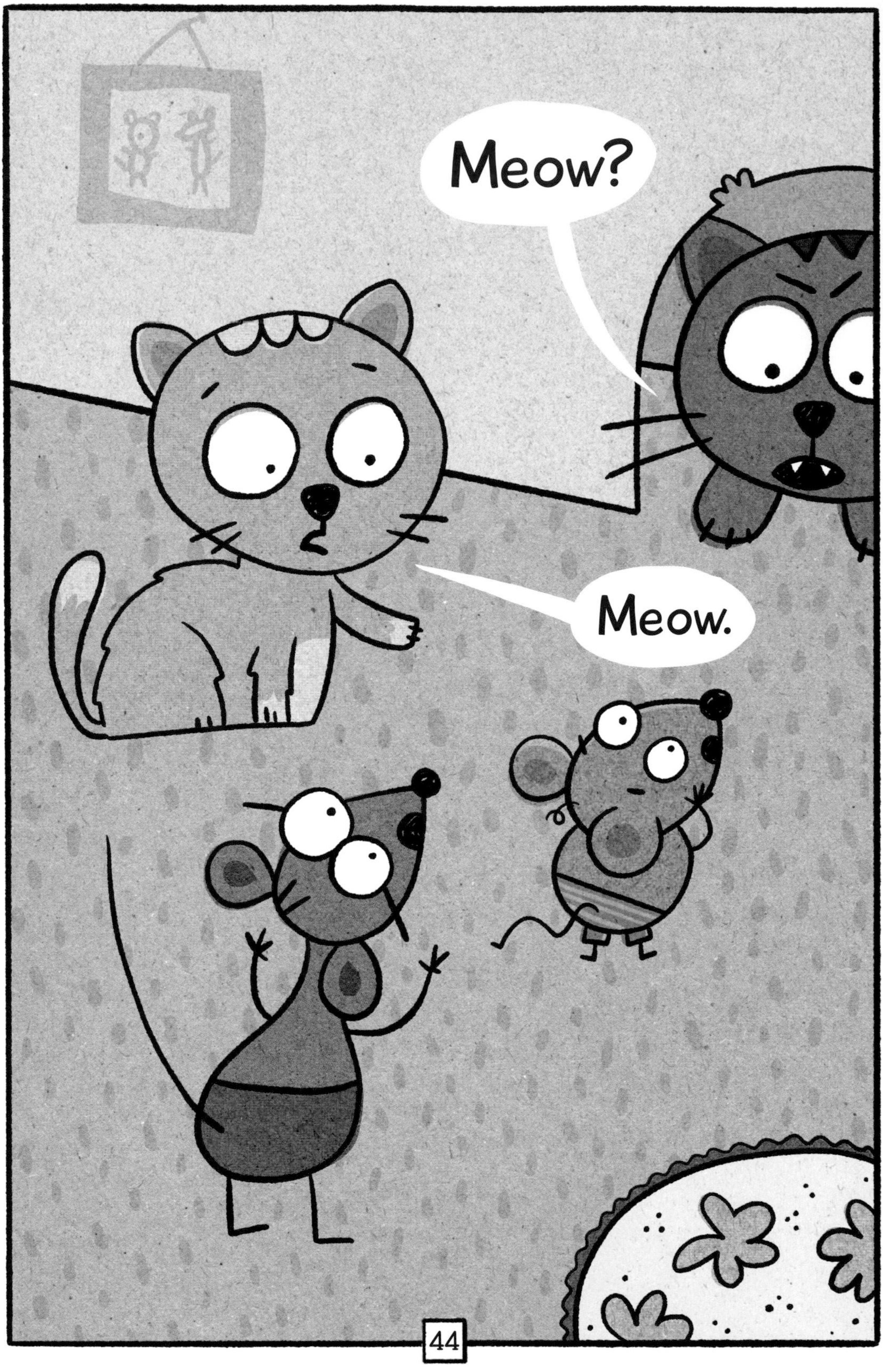
Meow?
Meow.

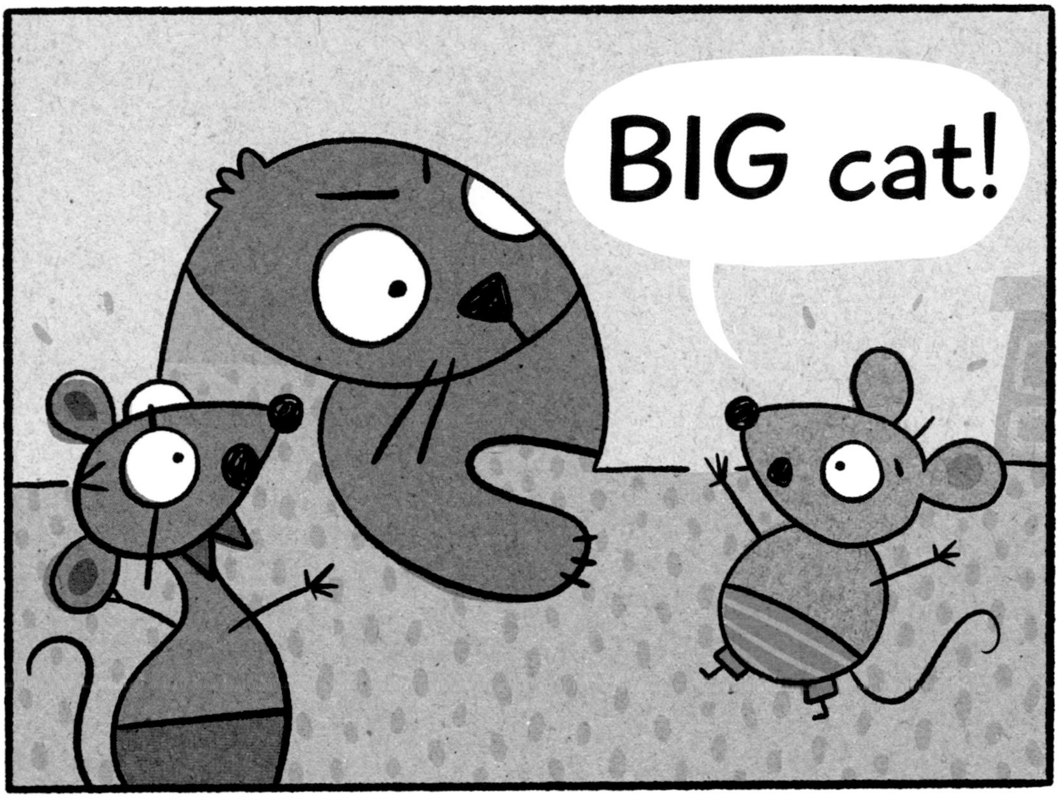
BIG cat!

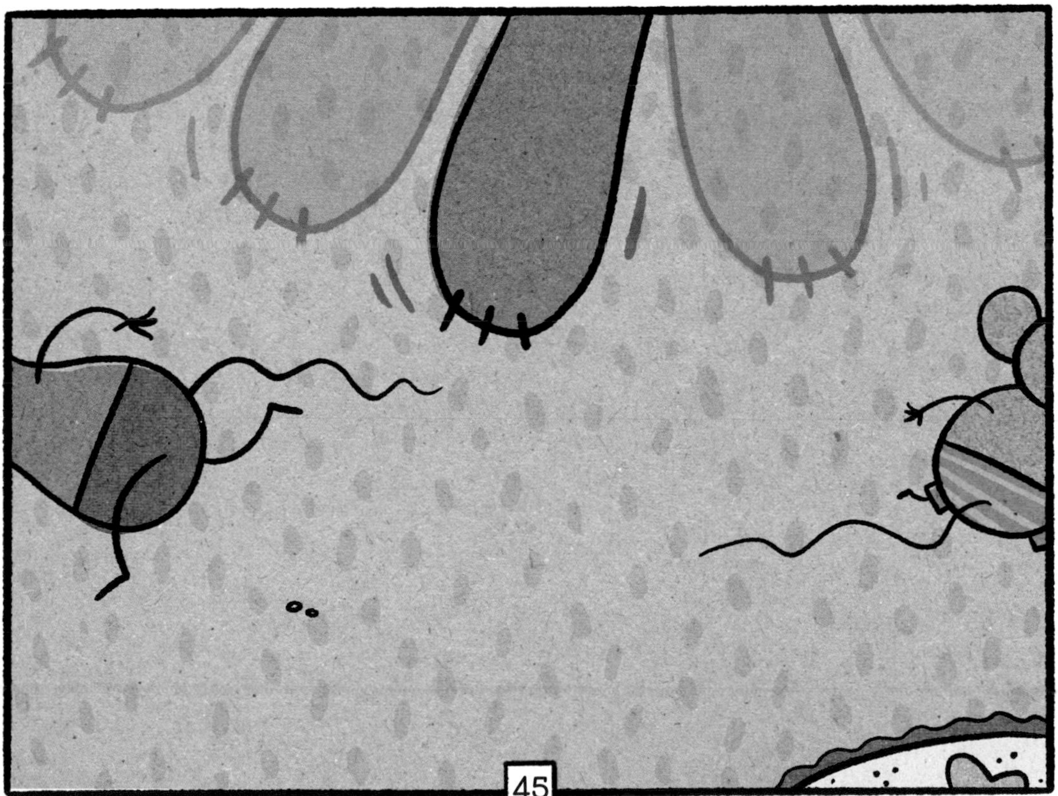

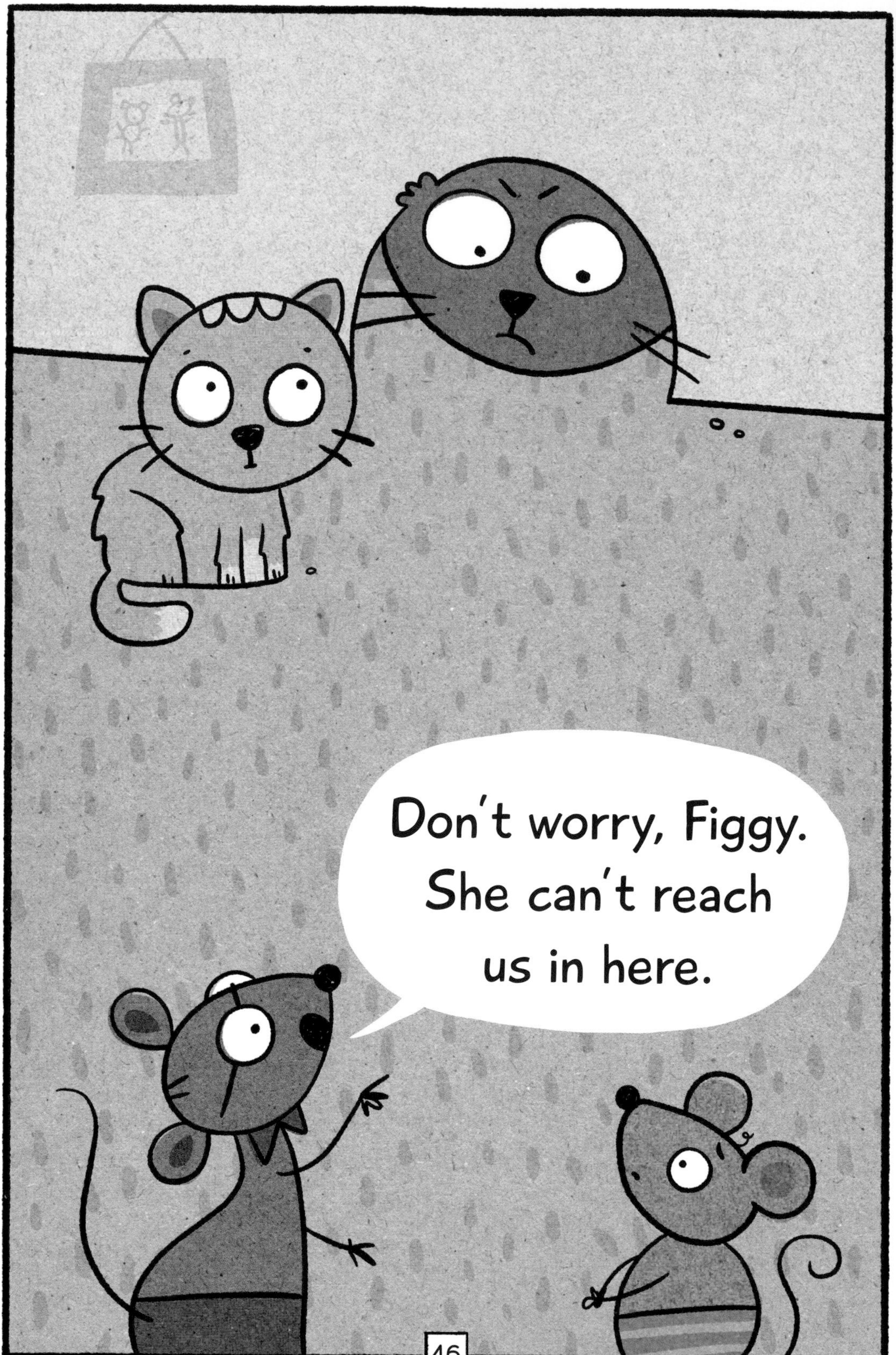
Don't worry, Figgy. She can't reach us in here.

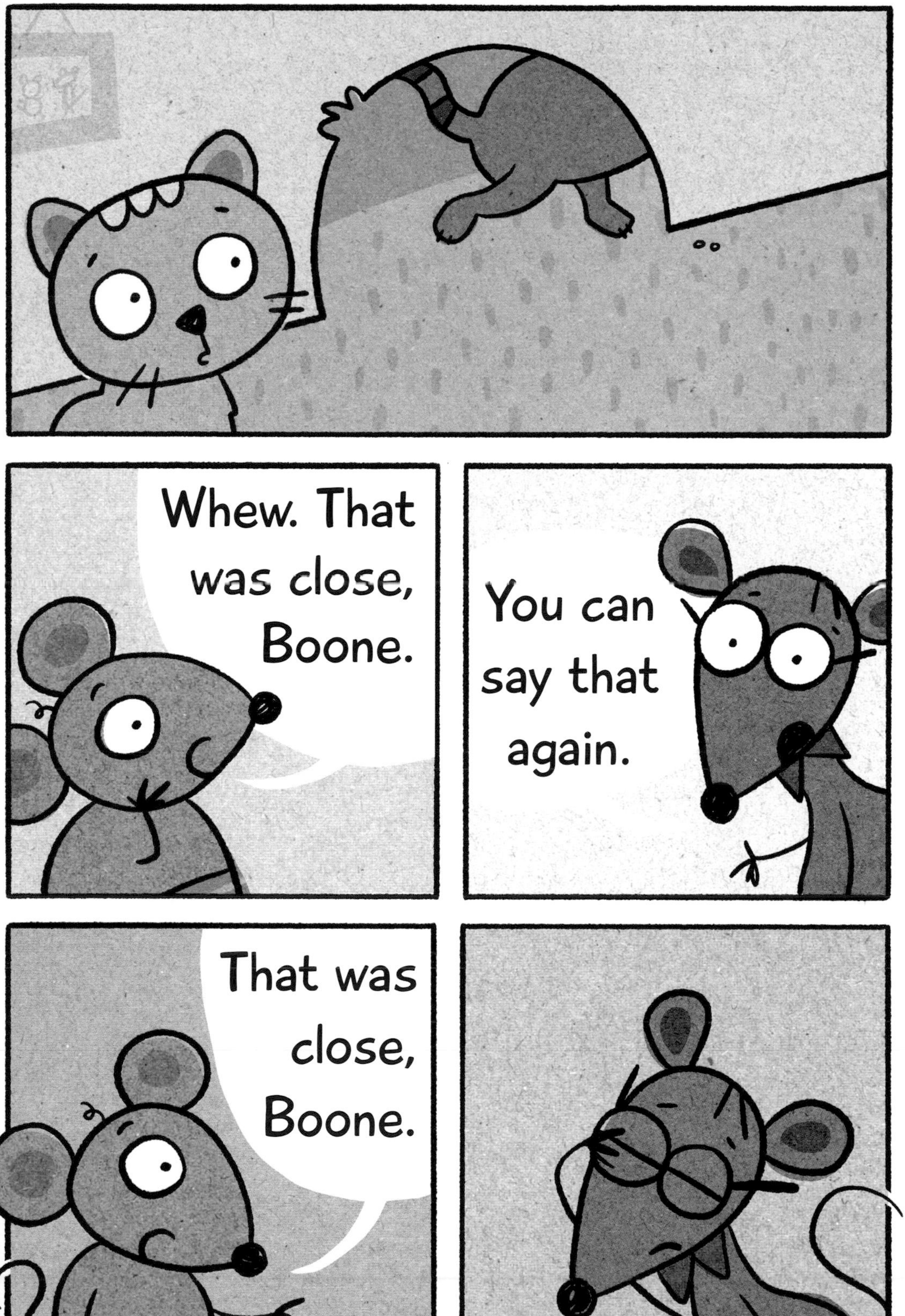
Whew. That was close, Boone.
You can say that again.
That was close, Boone.

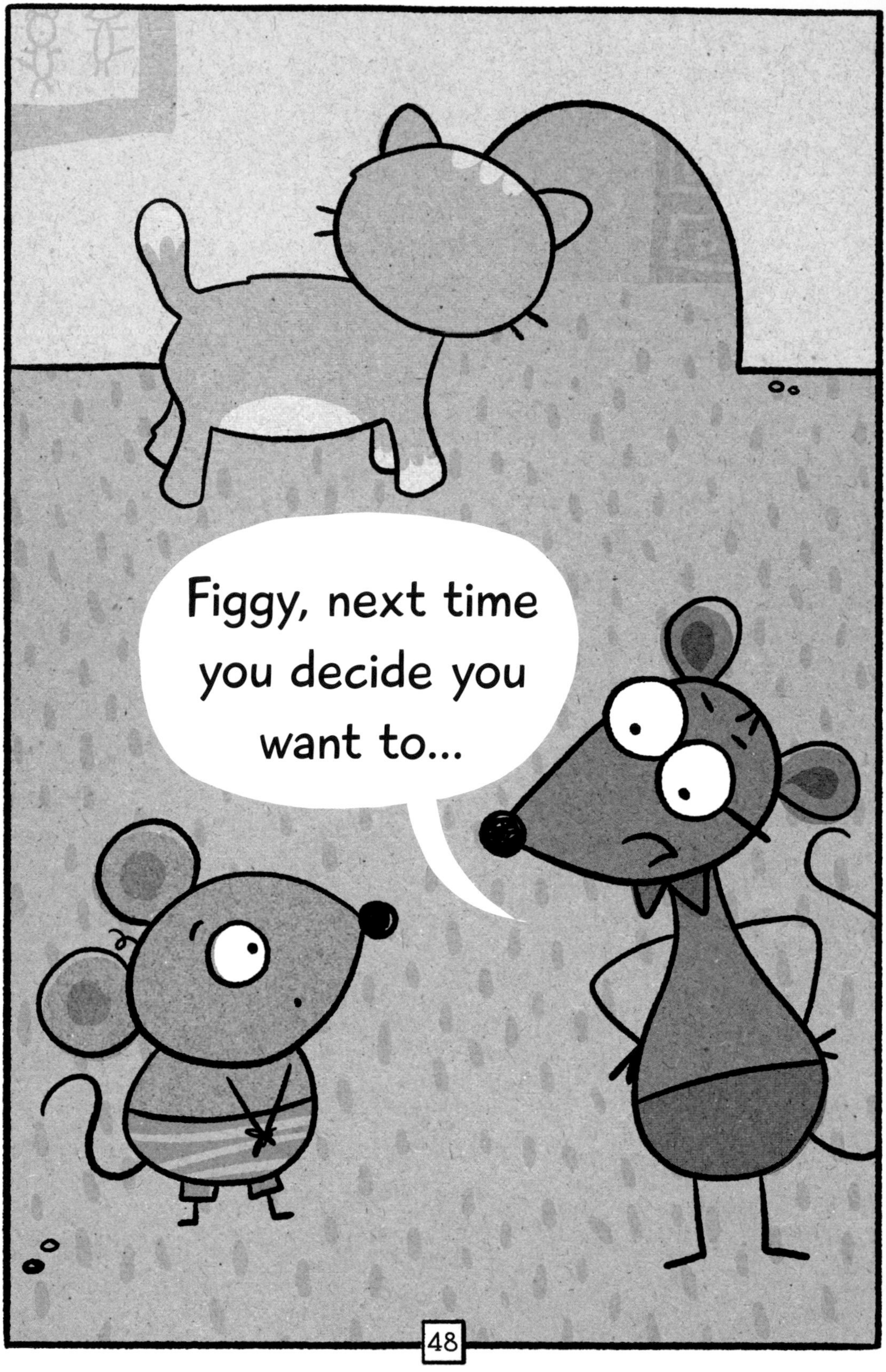
Figgy, next time you decide you want to...

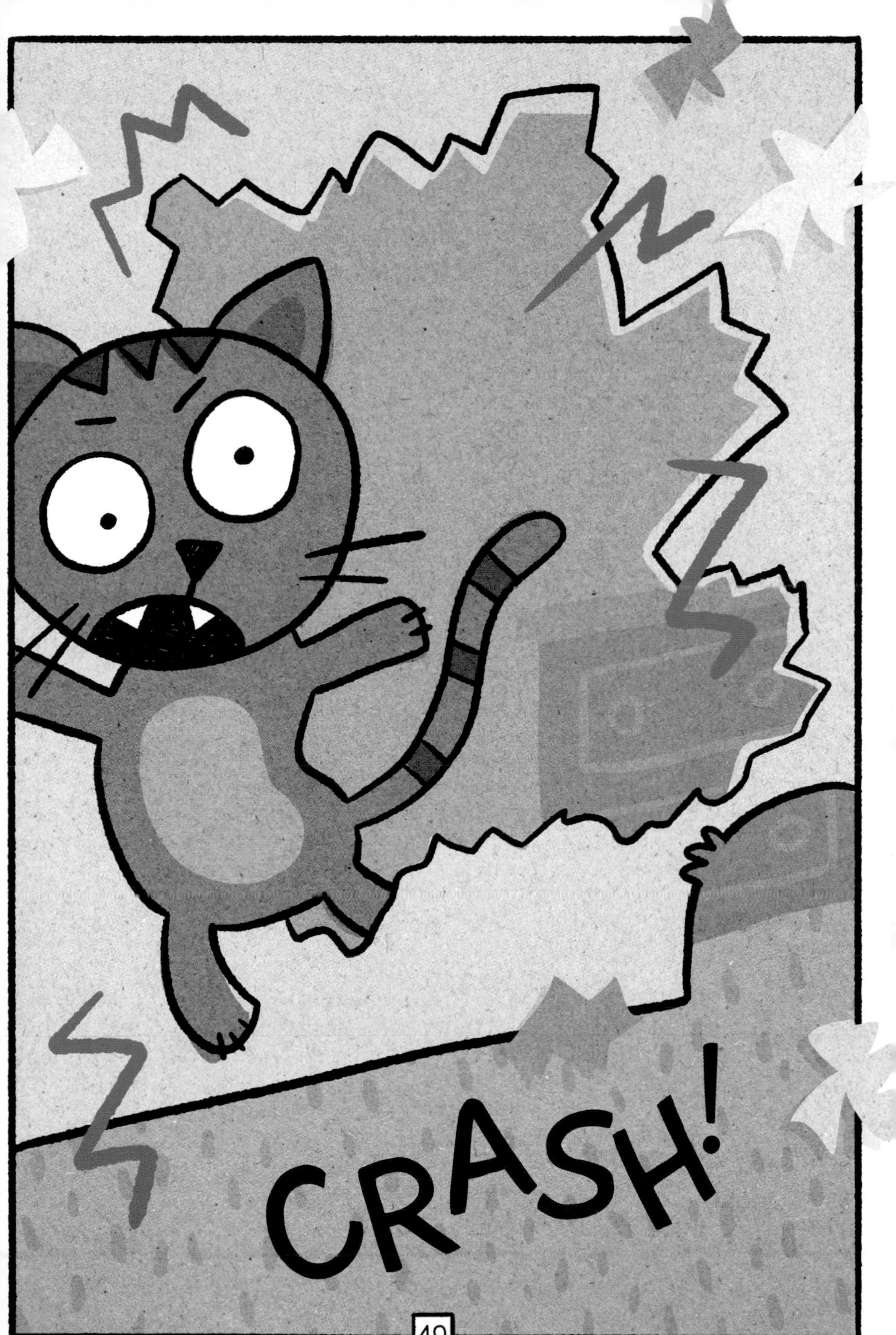
CRASH!

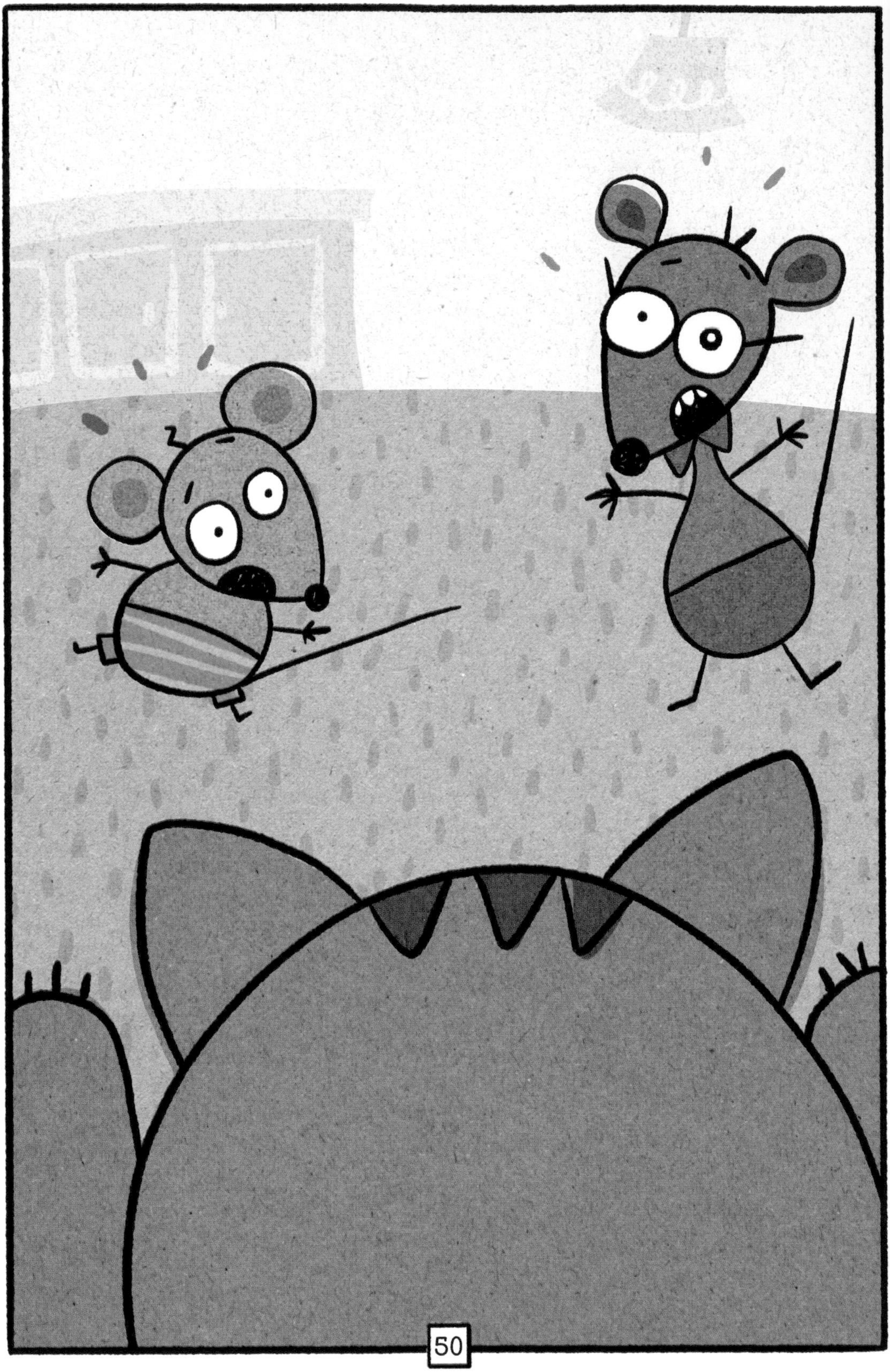

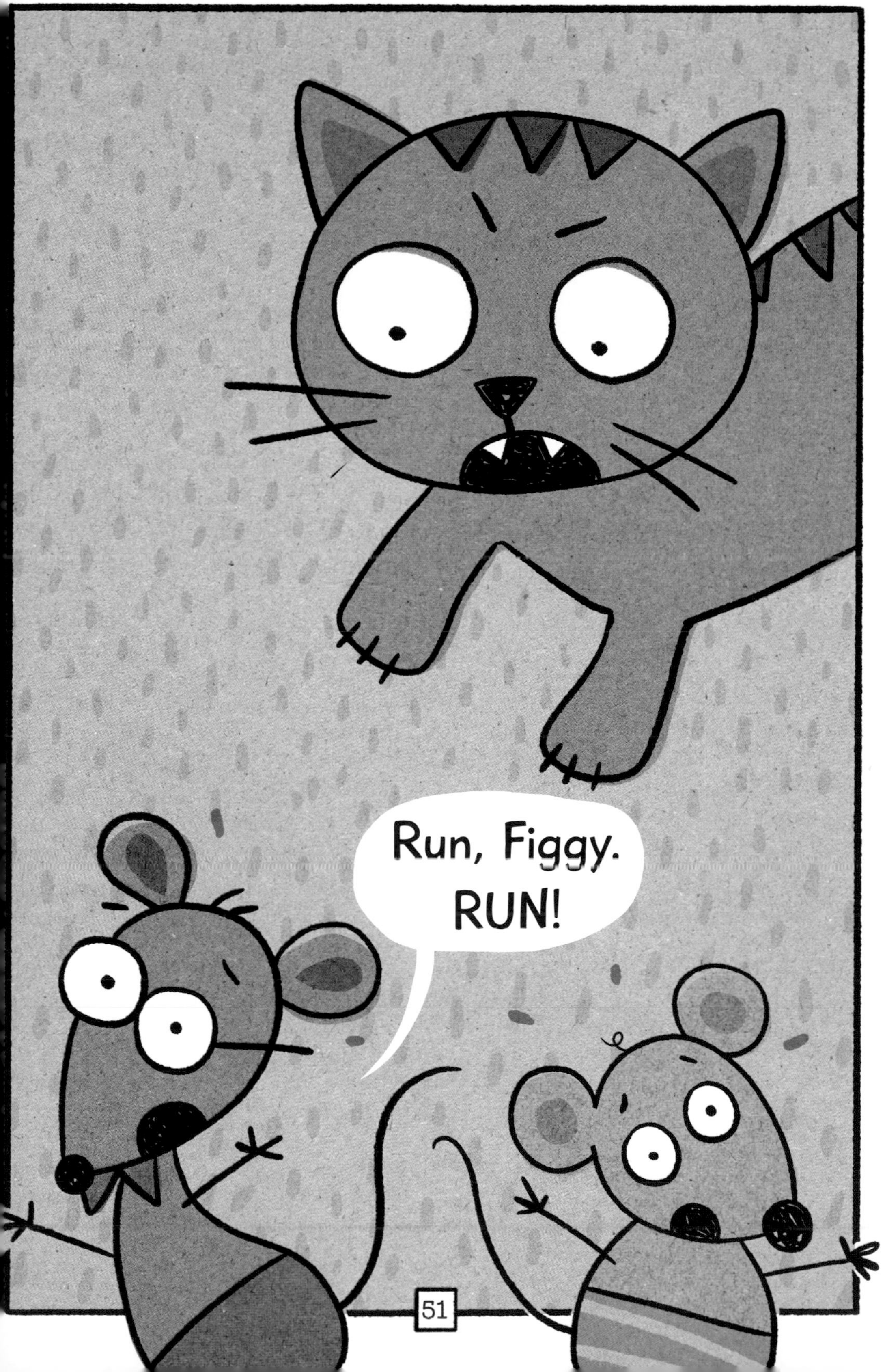
Run, Figgy. RUN!

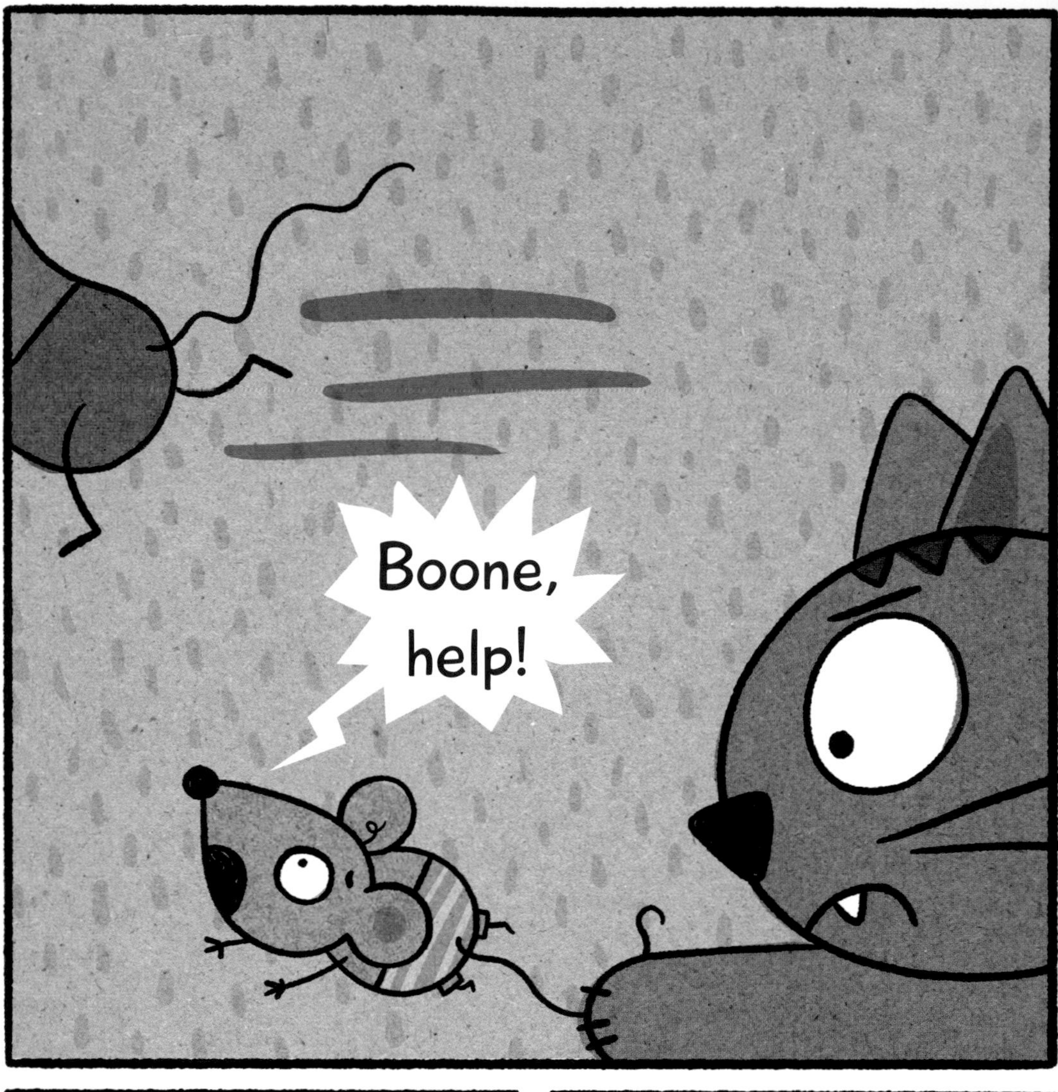
Boone,
help!

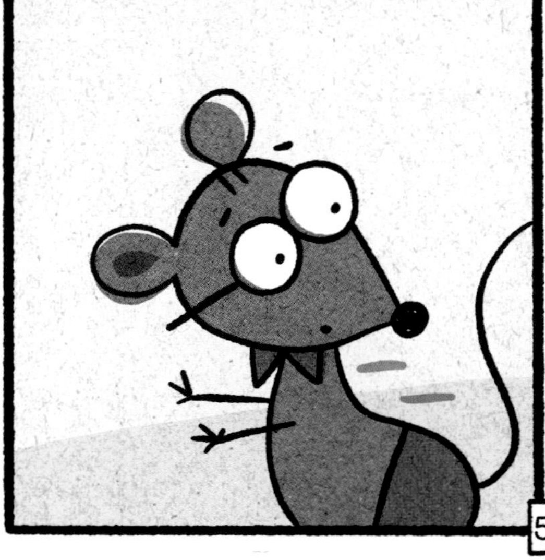

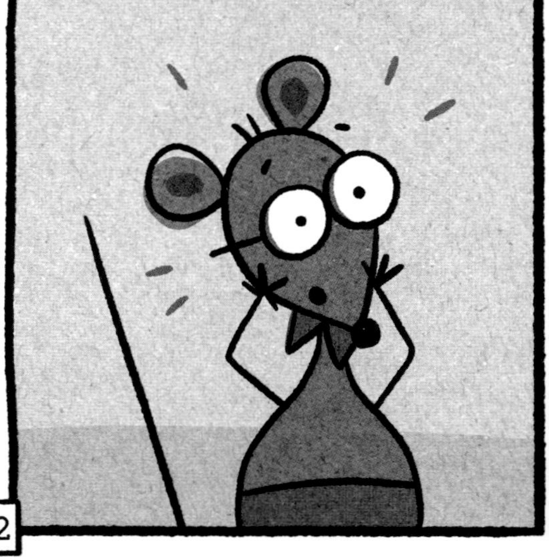

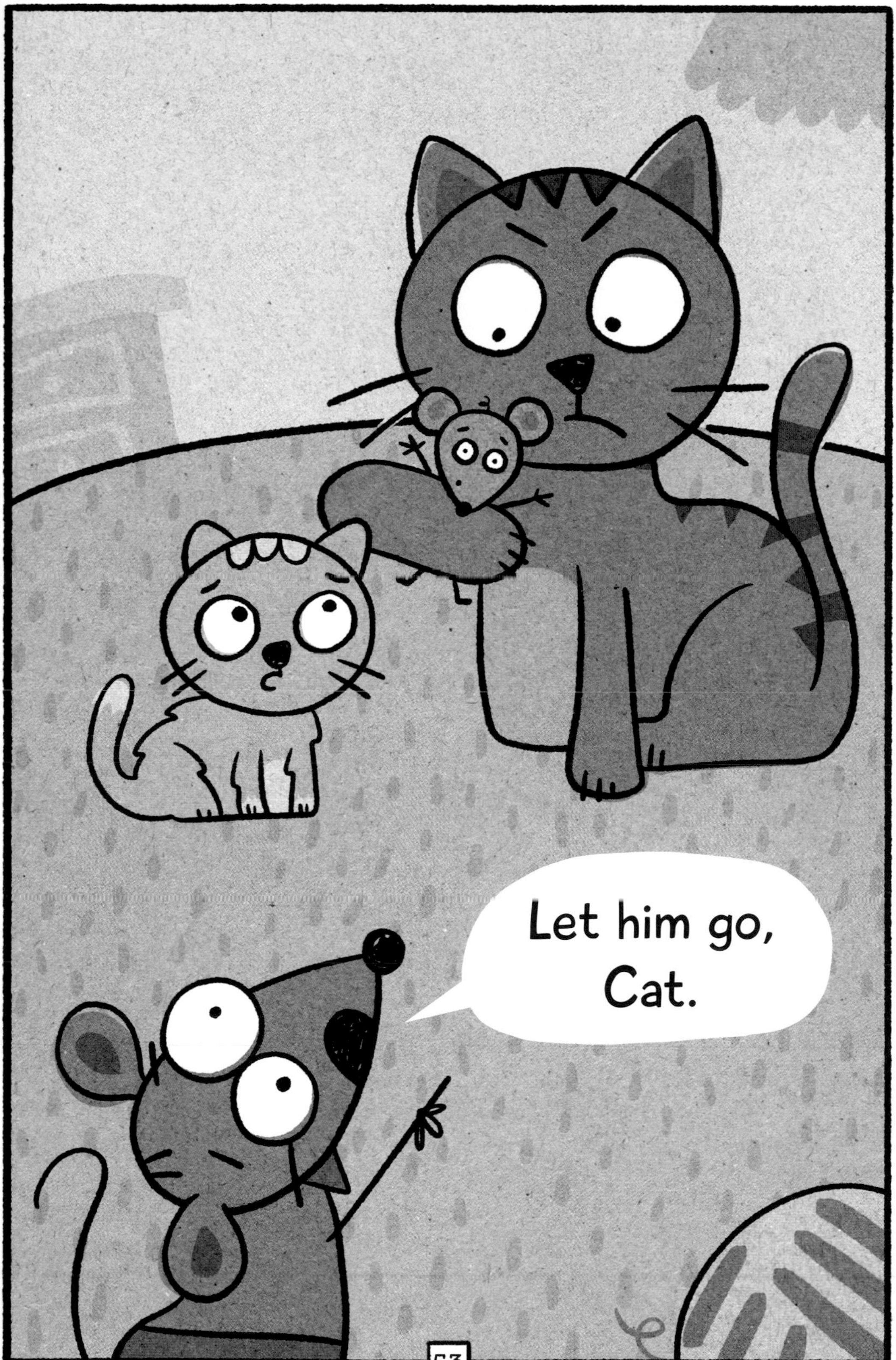
Let him go, Cat.

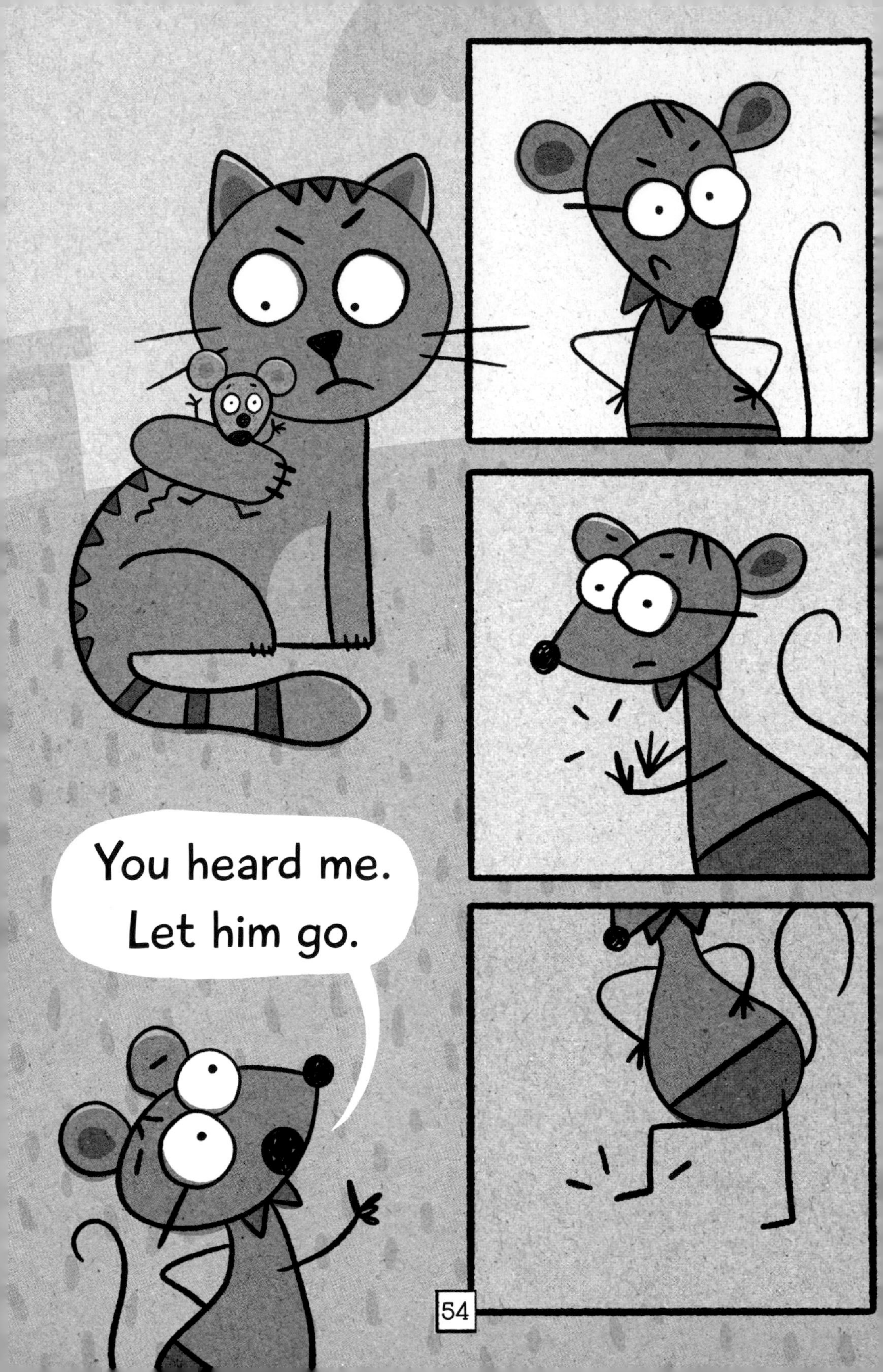
You heard me.
Let him go.

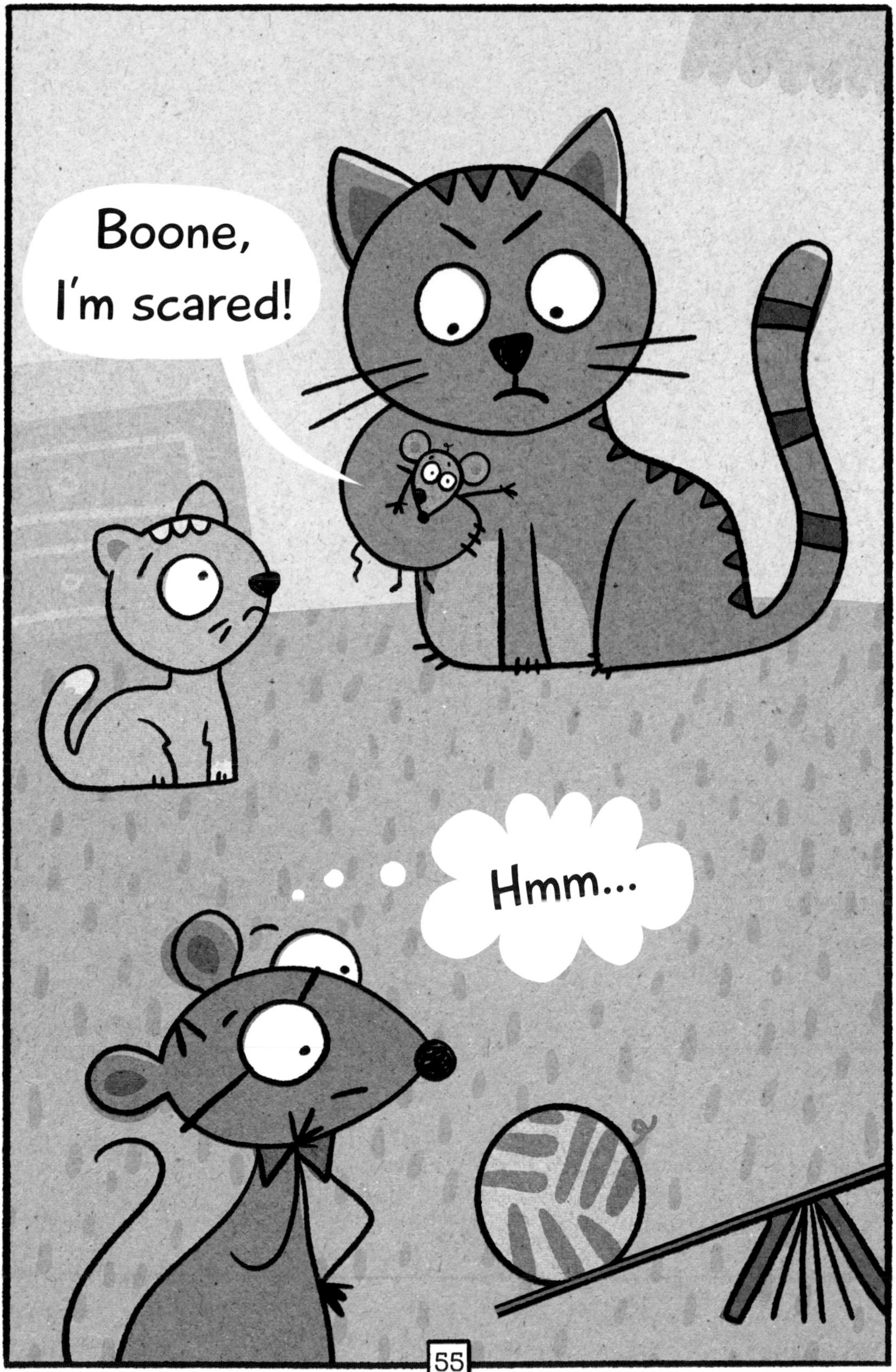
Boone,
I'm scared!
Hmm...

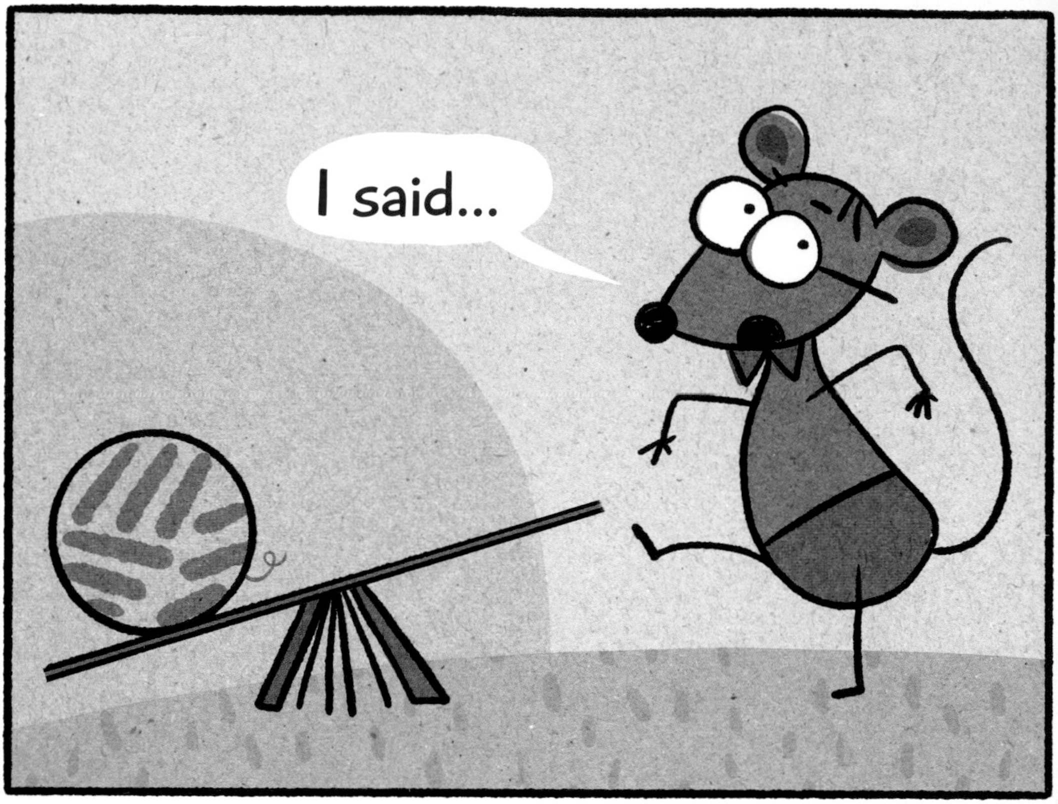
I said...

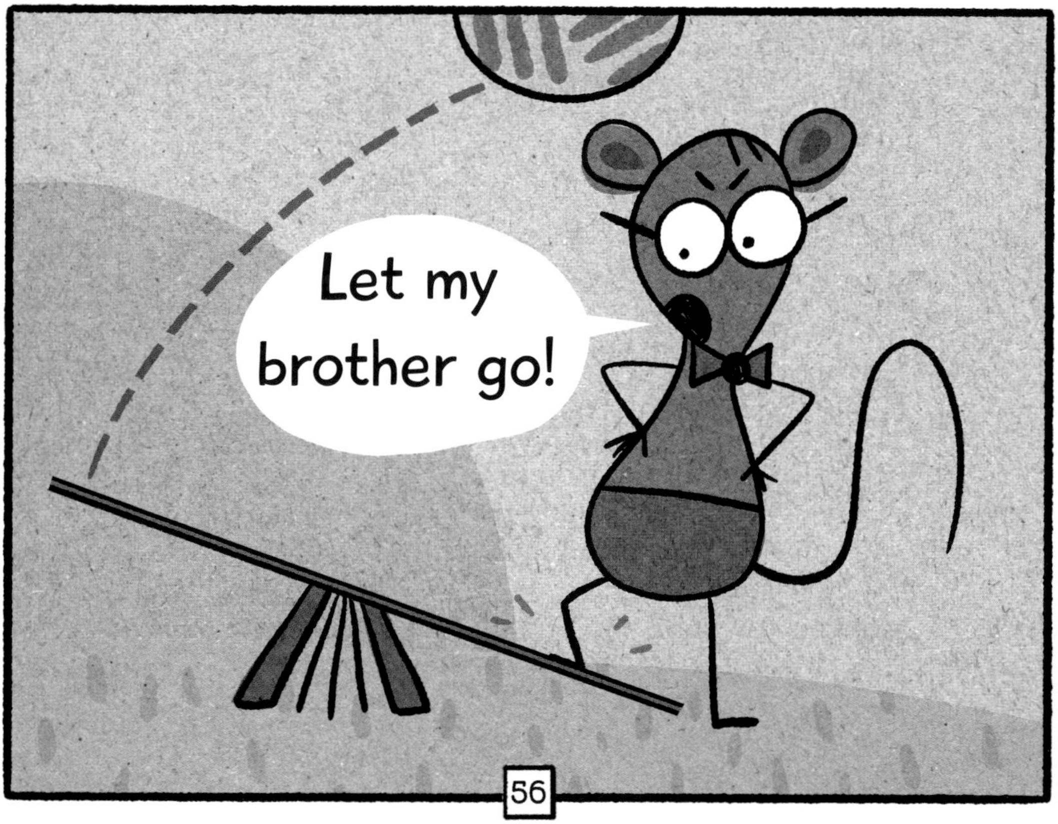
Let my brother go!

THUMP

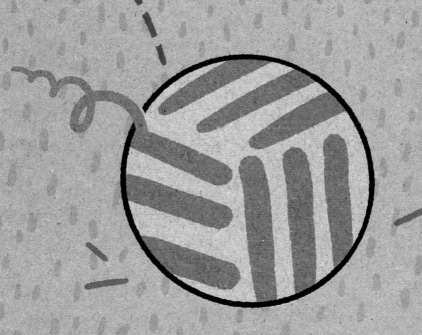

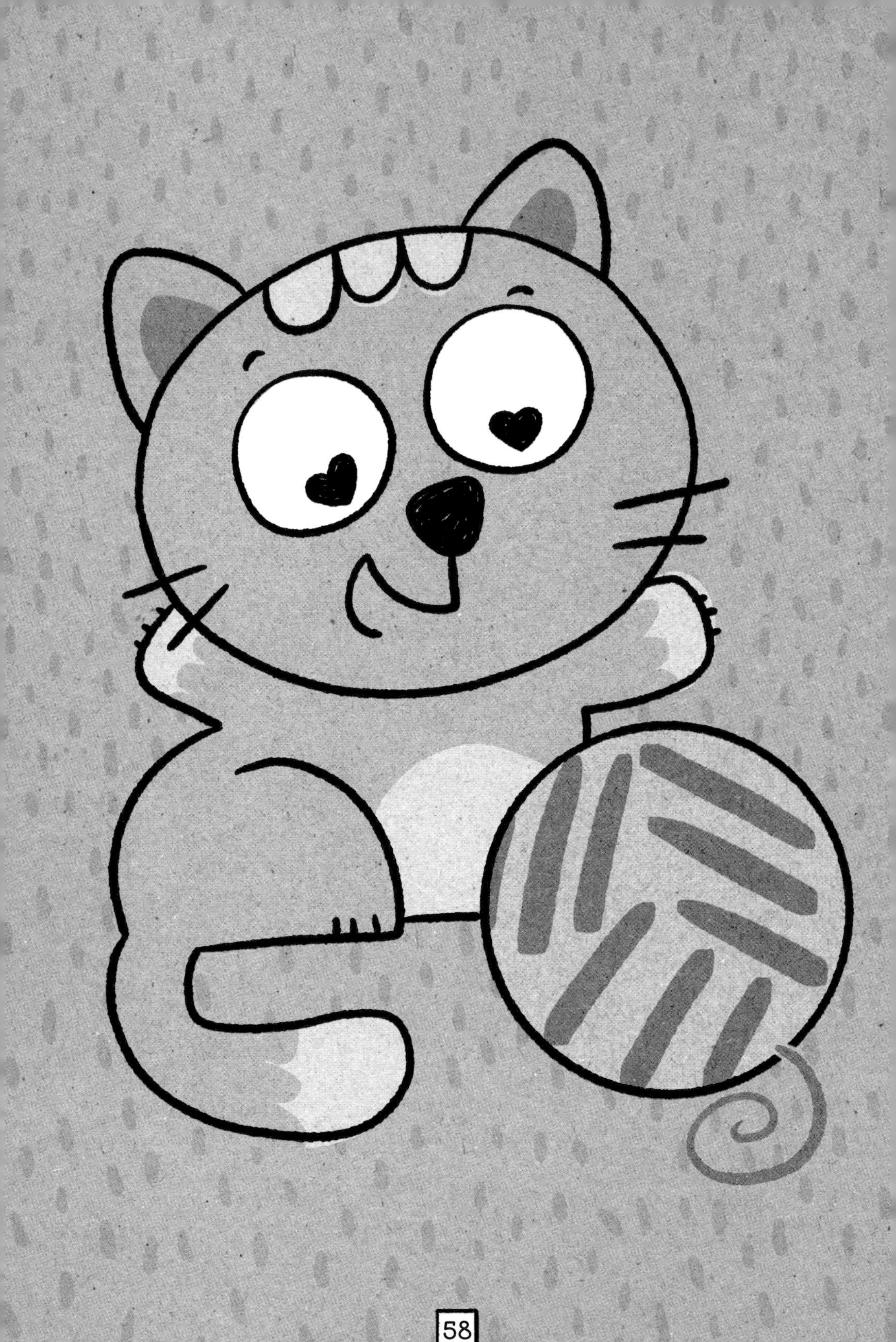

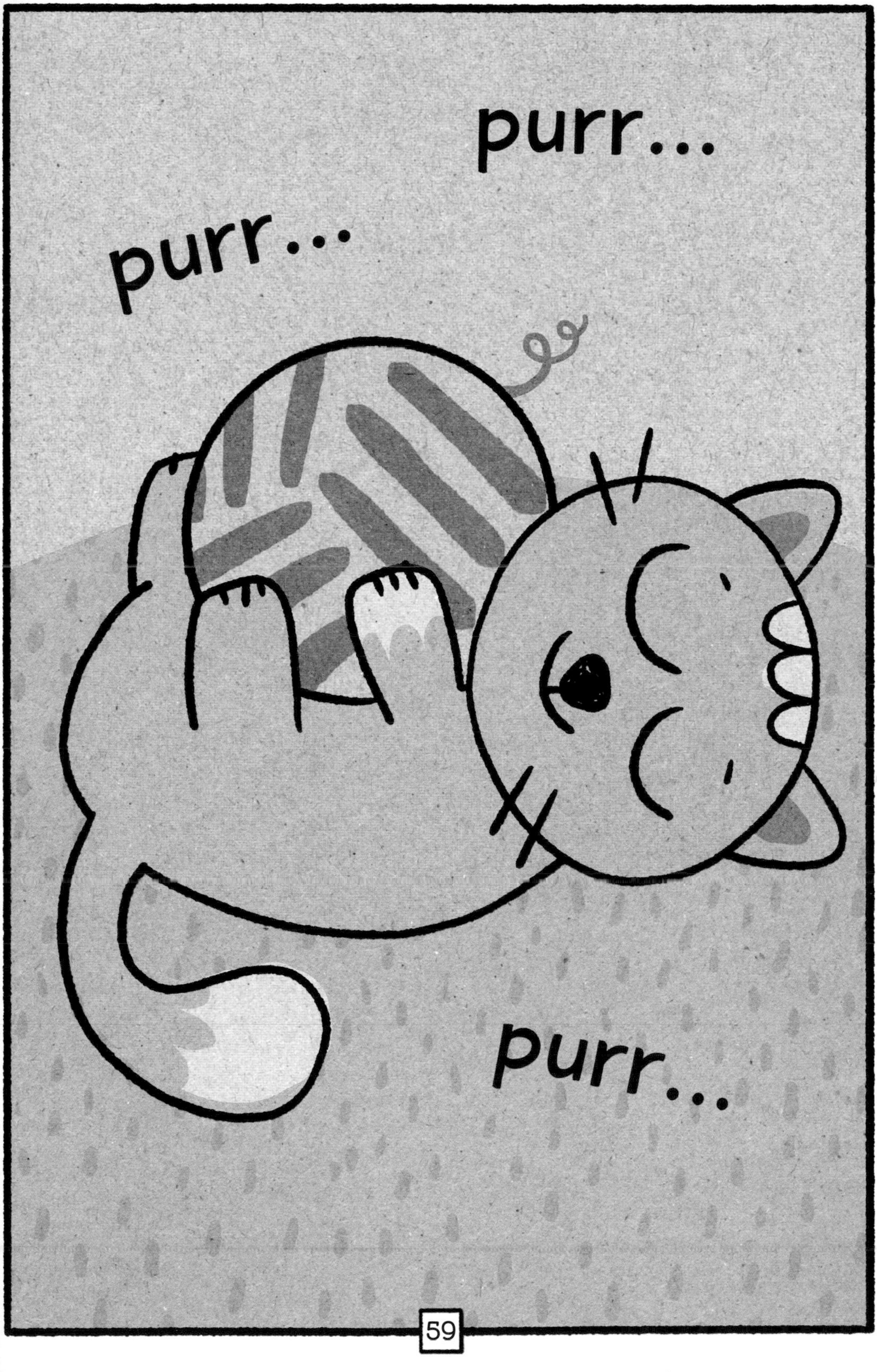
purr...
purr...
purr...

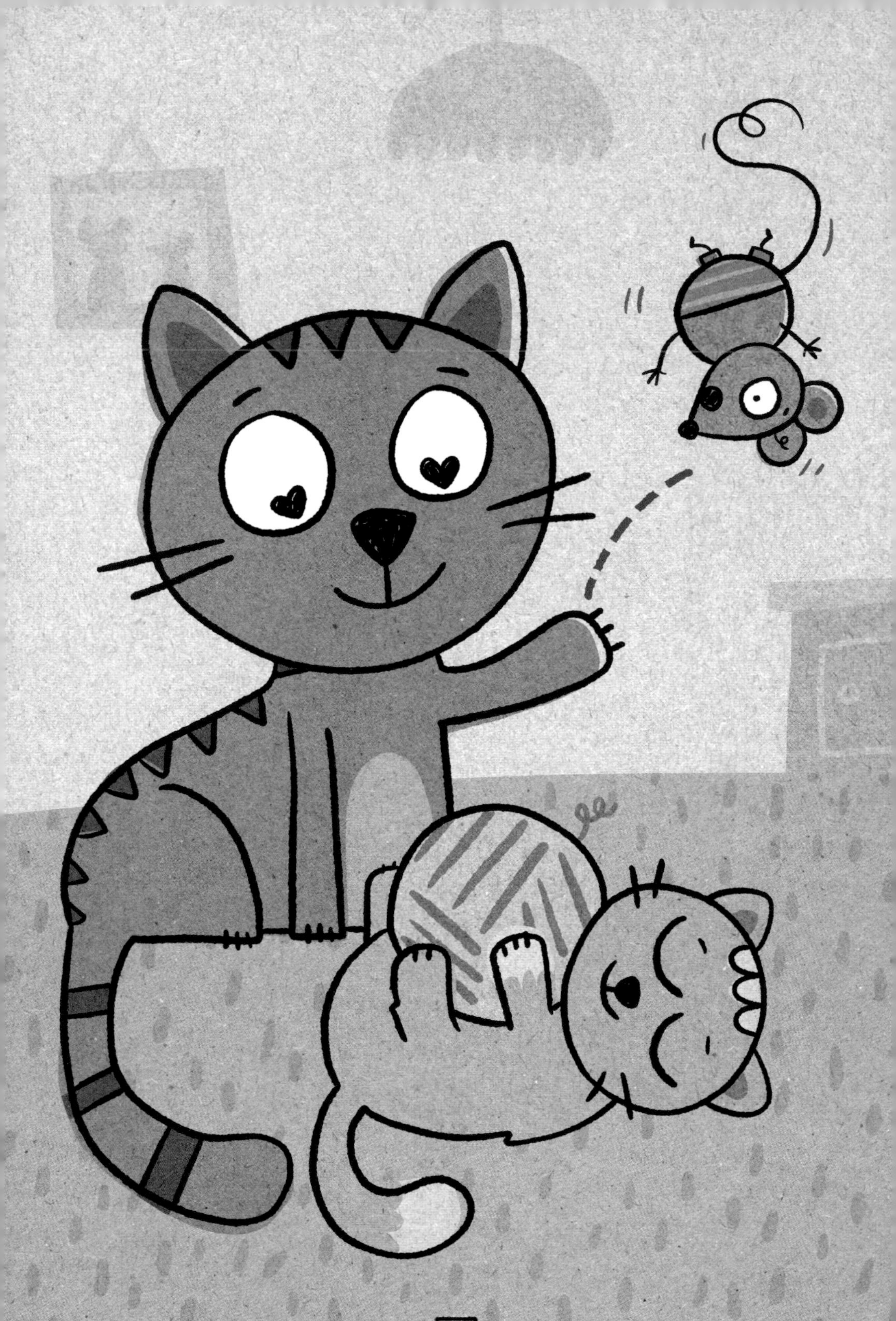

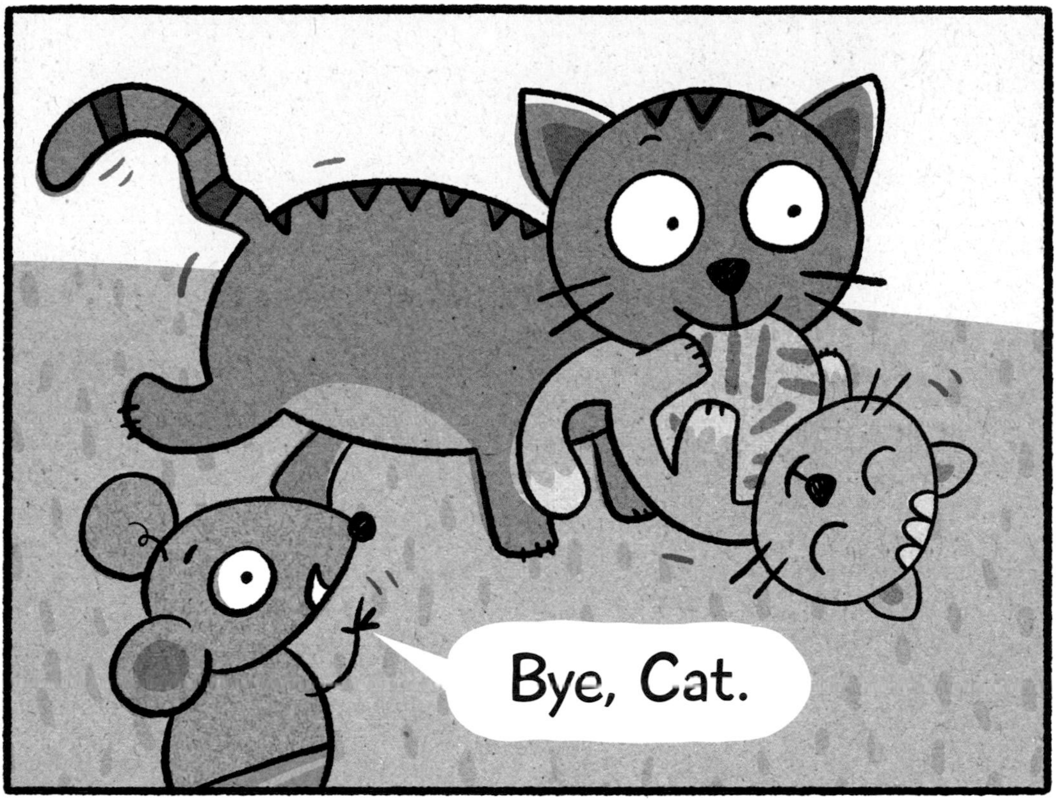
Bye, Cat.

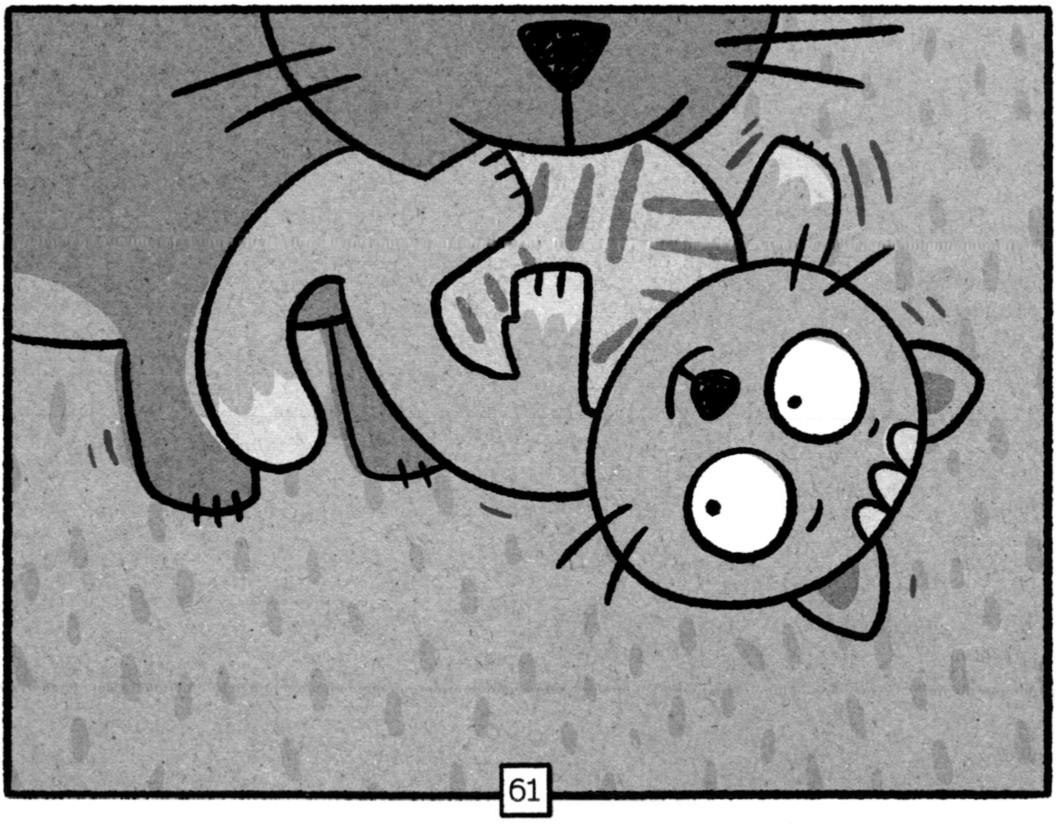

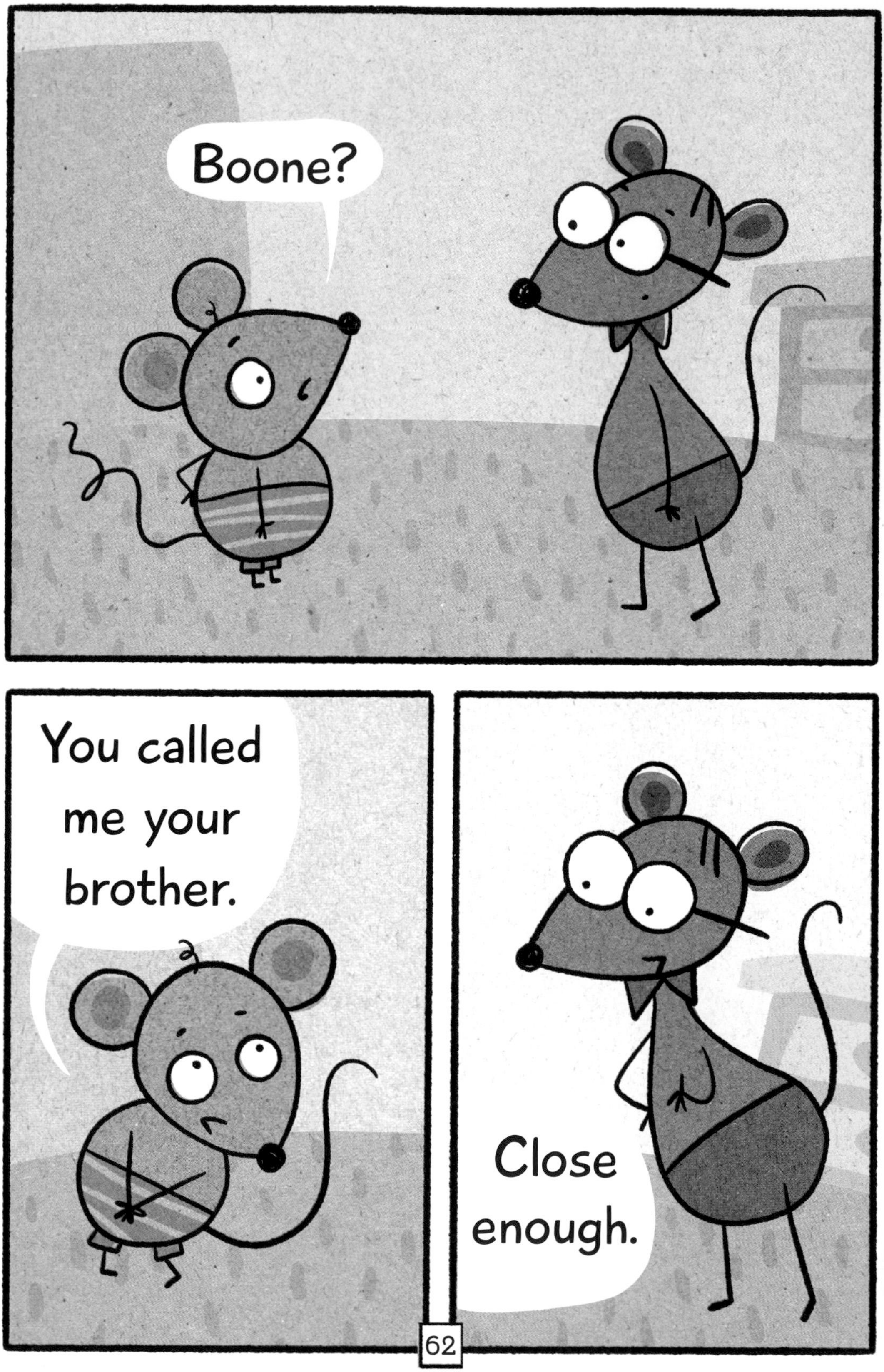
Boone?
You called me your brother.
Close enough.